Alice in the Know

Books by Phyllis Reynolds Naylor

Shiloh Books
Shiloh
Shiloh Season
Saving Shiloh

The Alice Books
Starting with Alice
Alice in Blunderland
Lovingly Alice
The Agony of Alice
Alice in Rapture, Sort Of
Reluctantly Alice
All But Alice
Alice in April
Alice In-Between
Alice the Brave
Alice in Lace
Outrageously Alice
Achingly Alice
Alice on the Outside
The Grooming of Alice
Alice Alone
Simply Alice
Patiently Alice
Including Alice
Alice on Her Way

The Bernie Magruder Books
Bernie Magruder and the Case of the Big Stink
Bernie Magruder and the Disappearing Bodies
Bernie Magruder and the Haunted Hotel
Bernie Magruder and the Drive-thru Funeral Parlor
Bernie Magruder and the Bus Station Blowup

Bernie Magruder and the Pirate's Treasure
Bernie Magruder and the Parachute Peril
Bernie Magruder and the Bats in the Belfry

The Cat Pack Books
The Grand Escape
The Healing of Texas Jake
Carlotta's Kittens
Polo's Mother

The York Trilogy
Shadows on the Wall
Faces in the Water
Footprints at the Window

The Witch Books
Witch's Sister
Witch Water
The Witch Herself
The Witch's Eye
Witch Weed
The Witch Returns

Picture Books
King of the Playground
The Boy with the Helium Head
Old Sadie and the Christmas Bear
Keeping a Christmas Secret
Ducks Disappearing
I Can't Take You Anywhere
Sweet Strawberries
Please DO Feed the Bears

Alice in the Know

PHYLLIS REYNOLDS NAYLOR

Atheneum Books for Young Readers
NEW YORK · LONDON · TORONTO · SYDNEY

Atheneum Books for Young Readers
An imprint of Simon & Schuster Children's Publishing Division
1230 Avenue of the Americas
New York, New York 10020

Book design by Ann Zeak
The text for this book is set in Berkeley Old Style.
Manufactured in the United States of America
First Edition
2 4 6 8 10 9 7 5 3 1
Library of Congress Cataloging-in-Publication Data
Naylor, Phyllis Reynolds.
Alice in the know / Phyllis Reynolds Naylor.—1st ed.
p.   cm.
Summary: Alice fills the summer before her junior year of high school
with a job at the mall, hanging out with her friends, and wishing she
had a bigger family.
ISBN-13: 978-0-689-87092-7
ISBN-10: 0-689-87092-2
[1. Family life—Maryland—Fiction. 2. Stores, Retail—Fiction.
3. Friendship—Fiction. 4. Maryland—Fiction.] I. Title.
PZ7.N39689Ali 2006
[Fic]—dc22   2005020514

To my granddaughter Sophia, with love

Contents

Hired

My knees were red from kneeling at my bedroom window, but I was obsessed. Elizabeth's family was having a reunion, and I couldn't stop watching.

For three days there had been a half dozen cars parked across the street. Relatives spilled onto the porch and steps, playing croquet in the side yard and badminton out front. A boy about twelve started a water fight with the hose, and all the cousins joined in, grandparents cheering them on from the porch.

I'd watched one of the uncles swing Liz's little brother around by his ankles. I'd seen an aunt braiding a new twist in Elizabeth's hair. Liz whispering to cousins under the linden tree at the curb. And I'd wanted it to be *me* surrounded by relatives. *Me* laughing and teasing and sharing secrets.

My mother's closest relatives were in Chicago.

Dad's were in Nashville, and Sylvia's were out west. All over the map, that's what we were— spread so far apart, we rarely saw each other. How sad is *that*?

Look what I've been missing, I thought, as Liz hugged everyone good-bye and people packed up to go home. *I* would have loved to have a gang of cousins to hang out with—more siblings, at the very least.

"Why couldn't you have been triplets?" I groused to Les when I finally went downstairs. Les doesn't live here anymore, but he stops by for dinner whenever he can.

"What?" said Les. "Can't get enough of me, huh?"

We'd had a barbecue out back the day before, and I'd gone with Dad and Sylvia to watch fireworks at the Mall. I'd liked sitting there on the blanket between them, enjoying the July night, the Washington Monument lit with flood lamps against the dark sky. But Liz, I knew, was there in the crowd with several dozen relatives, and I felt a little cheated that the rest of the people I love— *my* people, I mean—lived so far away.

Grow up, I told myself. Dad and Lester had done their best to raise me, and now I had Sylvia to fill in for the mom I'd lost. I thought of the way Les and Dad and I used to cook dinner together; of

Dad and Les teaching me to drive; of Sylvia helping me buy a dress and Dad letting me work for
him during the summer. Small family or not, they
were always there for me. So when I walked into
the kitchen for supper, I said, "I just want to thank
you, Dad, for letting me work at the Melody Inn.
It sure saves a lot of hassle."

Dad smiled at me and stabbed a chunk of
melon. "You're welcome," he said. "But you
know . . . I've been thinking . . . it would be good
for you to work someplace else for the rest of the
summer if you can find something."

"*What?*" I choked.

"March to a different drummer," he said.

I could only stare. Dad is manager of the music
store over on Georgia Avenue, and I'd been working there part-time ever since we moved to Silver
Spring.

"You mean . . . I'm being fired?" I cried.

"Of course not. We could still use you some
Saturdays and sale days if you're free, but it might
do you good to work for someone else for a
change."

"*Why?* Haven't I been doing a good job?" I'd
been running the little Gift Shoppe there at the
store all by myself on Saturdays. It's the counter
under the stairs to the second floor where we sell
all kinds of musical stuff—Mozart mugs and

Chopin scarves plus jewelry with a musical motif. I knew the merchandise! I could handle the cash register! "Are you hiring somebody new?" I asked.

"Yeah, Al," Les cut in. "He's outsourcing your job. Someone over in India's going to be running the Gift Shoppe on eBay."

"*What?*" I screeched.

"He's kidding," said Dad. "But you can't see what the rest of the world is like if you spend your spare time working for me."

"If you want me to see what the rest of the world's like, Dad, send me to Paris!" I said. "Let me work at a sidewalk café! Let me work at a bookstore in London!"

Dad smiled. "No such luck. But if you can find a job somewhere else this summer, go for it."

"Dad, it's *July!*" I protested.

"Yeah, it's a little late for that," said Lester. "She should have started looking in March."

"I realize that," said Dad. "If nothing turns up, you still have your job at the Melody Inn. But if you do find something, it won't be hard to get someone to take your place at the store."

"Thanks a lot!" I said, and glared down at the potato salad on my plate. The good jobs were already taken! Pamela was working at Burger King; Liz was helping out at a day camp; Patrick was doing grunt work for a landscaper; and all my other friends had found jobs at Montgomery Doughnuts or Sears or the Autoclean or something.

It was Gwen who had the choicest job of all, and she wasn't even getting paid: She was working as a student intern for a new program at NIH—the National Institutes of Health—a one-of-a-kind job due to her grades and her interest in biology. There was no way in the world I could do something like that.

After dinner I called everyone I could think of and asked if they knew of any job openings where they worked. Zero, zip, zilch. It was turning out to be the Horrible Summer of My Sixteenth Year. Little did I know that: (1) it would be a far worse summer for someone else; (2) there would be two trips coming up—one happy, one sad; and (3) I would come to hate Brian Brewster with every cell of my body.

Partly because I was angry at Dad for even suggesting I get another job so late in the summer, and partly because I was sort of excited that he had, I got up early that Saturday, put on my best stretch top and chinos and a pair of string sandals, and drove to Wheaton Plaza. Scary as it was, there were sixty or more stores with dozens of possibilities. My new boss could be in his late twenties and single; I could be helping customers select from the latest novels; maybe I'd be working in a jewelry store with a uniformed cop at the door; or I could be dressing mannequins in a store window. Suddenly almost anything seemed more exciting and glamorous than selling underwear with BEETHOVEN printed on the seat of the pants.

I decided to start at one end of the mall and fill out an application at every store I'd consider working in—twenty, at least. Part of me wanted about twenty rejections to throw in Dad's face; the other part wanted to get hired and earn a lot more than he'd been paying me. What I really wanted, I guess, was to have enough money to pay for my own car insurance and gas and oil, so I could persuade Dad to buy me a used car for my junior year.

The first store wouldn't even give me an application. "Full up," the manager said. "Sorry."

"Come by around April of next year," a woman at The Limited said. "We won't be hiring again till spring."

"You can fill out an application if you like, but we're not hiring," said a third.

This was such a waste! Dad just comes up with these ideas about what will be *good* for me without any consideration for what *I* feel about it. Like that sex education class at church, even though I ended up liking it. But this string of refusals wasn't just a waste of time; it was an embarrassment.

How dumb can she be? the managers must have been thinking, my applying in July. I could hear a couple of clerks laughing when I left a store. No way was I going to go through this twenty times. I decided to pick a couple more places and then go home and tell Dad to forget it. You just don't give an employee one day's notice to find another job when she hasn't done anything wrong. I had a notion to demand two weeks' severance pay and then quit my job. If Dad was going to be my employer, he'd have to act like one. I'd tell him that.

I took the escalator up to the employment office at Hecht's and began filling out an application. I'd completed about three fourths of the page when I became conscious of a woman in a gray suit passing through the room and stopping behind me to look over my shoulder. I could feel my cheeks start to redden, sure I must have misspelled a word.

"When can you start?" I heard her say.

I turned and saw a Hecht's name tag on her jacket. "Excuse me?" I said.

She reached for my application and gave it the once-over. "Are you willing to do rack work?" she asked. "We need someone to free up our salesclerks so they don't have to spend so much time clearing out the fitting rooms. When are you available?"

"Uh . . . anytime, really," I said.

"Now?"

I swallowed. "Well . . . yes! But I need to call my stepmom first. I've got her car."

"Will transportation be a problem?" she asked.

"No. I can always take a bus."

"Okay. Finish filling out the form and then meet me in the women's department. That's the section downstairs for extra-large sizes," she said. "They're having a big sale, and the fitting rooms are piled high with clothes that need to go back on hangers. You'll be a floater. We'll use you in whatever department you're needed. Lauren!" she called to a woman behind a desk. "She needs to call home, then have someone bring her to the women's department." She shook my hand, and I read JENNIFER MARTIN on her name tag. "I hope things work out, Alice," she said.

"Thank you, Miss Martin," I said excitedly. "I do too!" I couldn't believe it! Hecht's! The biggest store in the mall. I suddenly wasn't angry at Dad anymore and called Sylvia to tell her what happened.

"Really?" she said. "That's wonderful! How long will you be there?"

"I don't know. I didn't ask," I told her. "Do you need the car?"

"Not till tomorrow."

"Thanks. I'll take the bus most days. I'm really psyched!" I said.

I realized when I got to the women's department that the supervisor in the gray suit would probably have hired anyone who had been filling out an application that morning, because the place was a madhouse—the annual post–Fourth of July sale.

Miss Martin met me there and introduced me to a woman named Estelle, who led me back to the fitting rooms. A line of women, size fourteen and up, were already waiting to get in, heaps of clothes draped over their arms. Dress hangers tried to snag me as I passed by in the narrow hallway, and I stared as a woman in pants and bra darted out of a fitting room, snatched another shirt off a rack, then hurried back to her cubicle.

Estelle waved one hand at the rack, almost hidden by clothes. "All of these need to go back in stock, the sooner the better," she said. "Button the buttons, reattach belts, straighten collars—make them look presentable. I'll come in from time to time to get the clothes you've finished and put them back out on the floor. Every time you get a chance, go into a fitting room between customers and bring out all the items that are piling up in there. Let me know if there's anything you don't understand."

"Okay," I said. *What's to understand?* I wondered. Anyone could button buttons, fasten belts. I reached for a shirt and began.

It was warm in the fitting room hallway. The air didn't seem to circulate, and it smelled of new fabric, old carpet, and perspiration. I wished I'd worn a tank instead of the stretch top, sneakers in place of sandals. I'd wanted to look older, more sophisticated, but every step in my string sandals let me know the straps were there.

I pushed the first shirt to one side and reached for a dress with a zillion buttons down the back, tiny cloth-covered buttons that were difficult to push through the holes. One . . . two . . . three . . . Pants were next . . . clip to the hanger. Sundress . . . secure the straps.

Estelle came back a little later. "You'll have to work faster than that," she said. "When we're this busy, just do a few of the buttons and keep checking those fitting rooms. We're drowning back here!"

I'd been working only an hour when I thought I knew the meaning of the word *sweatshop*. My scalp was damp beneath my hair, my feet hurt. There was no place to sit, and women constantly jostled me as they shoved past with loads of garments to get the next fitting room.

"Honey, could you find me a size twenty-two in

pink?" someone asked, handing me a shirt, but I didn't know where to look and wandered out to find Estelle.

"Tell them to ask a salesclerk if they want another size or color," she said. "You don't have time for anything except getting clothes ready to go back on the floor."

I had started work about eleven, and it was now almost one thirty. I hadn't even gone to the restroom. I hadn't had a drink, hadn't sat down. . . .

For a brief moment I felt tears welling up in my eyes. This wasn't what I'd had in mind. I couldn't see anyone here in this hot hallway except women in their underwear grabbing things out of my hands. If I were Pamela, I'd be talking to friends who came along. If I were Elizabeth, I'd at least be outdoors. How could I spend my whole summer back here in this smelly hallway? I hadn't even asked what salary I was getting. Hadn't asked my hours. What if they wanted me to work evenings and I never got to see my friends at all?

"Alice?"

I turned to see a pretty twenty-something blonde. "Lunchtime," she said. "The super asked me to come get you. We've got forty minutes. I'm Ann."

"Oh, am I ever ready!" I said, and got my bag from beneath the cash register out front.

We went to the food court and got Chinese.

"My feet!" I said, kicking off my sandals. I could see the red lines left in my flesh.

"Ouch! That must hurt!" Ann said, wincing. "Wear comfortable shoes. That's the first thing I learned on this job."

"How long have you worked here?" I asked.

"Four years. I'm in evening wear. Taking business management and fashion courses. I'd like to move up to buyer eventually. Are you going into your senior year?"

"No. Junior."

She looked surprised. "Jennifer usually hires only seniors. More responsible, she says. But as you can see, we're desperate."

"That's supposed to make me feel good?"

Ann laughed and gave my arm a quick squeeze. "I just meant you're lucky. If you work fast and you're dependable, she'll probably keep you on. And once you start moving about the store— other departments—you won't feel so claustrophobic."

"I hope so," I said.

I tried to work faster that afternoon. I darted into each fitting room ahead of the customers, grabbed the clothes dropped on the floor or hanging on hooks, and was out again in seconds. Estelle gave me a full smile when she came back to collect what I'd finished.

"Now you're cooking!" she said. *In more ways than one,* I thought, wiping my sweaty forehead. Then she noticed I was working barefoot. "Uh-uh," she said. "There are straight pins on the floor. It's against company rules to go without shoes."

"Sorry," I said, and put my sandals back on my tortured feet.

It was about four when I sensed something going on. I had just taken a load of dresses out to the floor when a look passed between Estelle and one of the salespeople. A man in a blue Windbreaker, a walkie-talkie tucked in his belt, came striding up to the counter, exchanged a few words with Estelle, and went quickly over to a side entrance. Moments later he came walking back, gripping the arm of a woman who was protesting loudly. In minutes two security officers arrived, one of them a female who ushered her into a fitting room while the other one, a male, stood guard outside. I thought I recognized the red-haired woman—thought she'd been in a fitting room a half hour earlier—but I remembered her as a lot thinner.

I stared at Estelle.

Shoplifter? I mouthed, and she nodded.

Now the female officer inside the fitting room

was handing out garment after garment to the officer in the hallway. The shoplifter had two more pairs of pants under the baggy brown trousers she'd worn, four more tops under her navy blue shirt.

Two Montgomery County policemen arrived on the scene, and the woman sat on the stool in the fitting room, arms folded defiantly across her chest, and only pressed her lips tightly together and shook her head as the police questioned her. Finally they led her away as customers stared.

"How did she think she was going to get out of the store without tripping the security sensors?" I asked Estelle.

"She didn't, but she had an accomplice waiting for her in a car just outside the entrance. They'd talked to each other by cell phone. A security guard got suspicious and nabbed her when she came out."

"Wow!" I said.

"A little excitement to liven up your first day," Estelle told me.

Dad and Sylvia were out for the evening when I got home, so I called Liz and Pamela to come over and have dinner with me. I was soaking my feet in a basin of water when they arrived, and I propped them one at a time on Liz's lap while she massaged lotion into all the dents left by my string sandals. With her long dark hair and eyelashes, she looked like a storybook figure in a sultan's harem, rubbing her master's feet. Pamela, on the other hand, with her short blond hair, could have been Peter Pan as she boiled tortellini on the stove and opened a jar of sauce.

"I work on the lower level, Alice! The Burger King's just outside of Hecht's!" Pamela said excitedly. "We can have lunch together!"

"Wish I worked at the mall too!" said Liz.

"No, you don't," said Pamela. "You wish Ross had gone back to Camp Overlook this summer and that you were both counselors there again."

Liz was quiet for a moment. "I guess that wasn't meant to be."

I studied her. "What do you mean?"

"We sort of agreed it's over."

"Liz!" said Pamela, turning.

"It's unfair to both of us, and we know it. He can't come down every time there's something special going on, and I can't go up to Philly. We're still going to e-mail and everything, but . . . Well, he purposely took that construction job this summer instead of applying for camp, and that made it pretty final."

"Oh, Liz," I said.

"I know. He's still probably the nicest guy I ever met. And maybe someday . . . Well, who knows?"

I sighed. *Everything* was changing. It was the first summer we were all working at different jobs. We wanted to do new stuff, meet new people, but at the same time we wanted to keep the old crowd going. When someone didn't show up for a night swim at Mark Stedmeister's or a game of miniature golf or for anything else we'd planned, we'd think, *Why did he have to take an evening job?* or *Didn't she know we were going to the movies?* Like they were traitors or something. And then, maybe next time, we'd be the ones who missed.

I put on my favorite CD, and we took our plates to the living room and ate on the rug around the coffee table.

"It's a big, scary year coming up, you know?" Pamela said. "We've got to start thinking about SATs, college, sex. . . ."

"What?" I said. "You've got a timetable for *that*?"

"No, but I don't want to reach eighteen, either, and find out I'm the only virgin on the block," she said.

Liz and I broke into laughter. "So what are you going to do? Take a poll?" asked Liz.

Pamela leaned back against the couch. "I just have the feeling that there's all this *living* to do, and I might be missing out on something. I want to squeeze in everything I can. Let's all plan to meet at Mark's pool every Monday night for the rest of the summer. That'll give us a chance to check up on what everyone's doing, and if anybody's got a wild and wonderful idea, we'll try it."

"Not necessarily!" Elizabeth said with a laugh. "But it would be great if we could all get together at a definite time once a week. We're so scattered." She glanced at me. "Maybe Patrick will show up too."

Patrick, my ex-boyfriend, the brain, was on an accelerated program and would graduate a year early. Not only was he going to summer school, but he was working for a landscaper, too. You never forget your first boyfriend, they say. But now that he and Penny—the girl who had stolen him from me—had broken up, he'd been going out with a new girl, Marcie, and I wondered if they were still an item. Of course, I'd dated and broken up with Sam Mayer since then, and Penny was dating Mark now, so I suppose anything could happen. There were changes going on all around us, and Mark's pool was our anchor, the one place we'd been meeting since seventh grade.

Couples had met there and split up. Kids had been celebrated, mortified, terrified, and yet we kept coming. Pamela had had potato salad dumped down her bikini bottom; I'd had to face my fear of the deep end; Liz had developed anorexia because of something a boyfriend said;

Patrick had embarrassed me by putting lemon halves on my breasts when I fell asleep on Mark's picnic table; Liz had learned to insert a tampon in Mark's bathroom. . . . We could almost write the history of our gang from all that had gone on at Mark Stedmeister's house.

"To summer!" I said, raising a glass of Diet Pepsi.

"To us!" said Liz, clinking mine.

2

Dinner for Three

Since neither I nor my three best friends—Pamela, Elizabeth, and Gwen—had a boyfriend at present, it made summer more simple. Comfortable. Easy. With all the energy I had to spare, I decided to focus my attention on Lester, who was dating a woman of color named Tracy.

I liked the way that rolled off my tongue when I talked about her to friends—"a woman of color"—because you could imagine any color at all, from antique ivory to coffee to ebony. "Woman of color" sounded mysterious, exotic, passionate and made "white" sound like mashed potatoes. Les was really serious about her, and if they married, I wanted it to be a strikingly elegant wedding, with everyone who was black coming in white and everyone who was white coming in black. Sylvia and I look great in black, by the way.

Before I left for Hecht's on Sunday, Les called and asked for me.

"Yeah?" I said, surprised.

"Sylvia told me about your new job," he said. "Nice going!"

"I thought so too!" I said.

"Listen, Tracy's cooking for me tonight, and we're inviting you over for dinner," he said.

I tried to let that soak in. His girlfriend was inviting *me* to an intimate dinner at Lester's apartment? "Just me?" I asked.

"Dad and Sylvia are going out with friends," he said.

"Well . . . sure! I don't get off till six, though," I told him.

"So come at six. They're going in Sylvia's car. Dad said you could drive his."

"Great!" I said. "See you!"

Funny how you can feel five years more mature just by driving to a new job with a dinner date waiting for you at the end of the day. Even if the date's with your brother. I could remember when Les would have gladly paid me to keep out of sight. When he didn't even want me *talking* to his girlfriends on the phone. Now I was invited to dinner!

The store had just opened when I got to

Hecht's, so the women's department wasn't packed with customers yet. Estelle showed me the different sections for sport clothes and dresses, for different brands and separate sizes. This time she let me bring clothes back out to the floor by myself when I could keep up with stuff from the fitting rooms, and I liked being out in the store area, helping direct customers to the right sections. Hourly, I blessed the person who invented sneakers.

Pamela came looking for me when she was on her lunch break, but I couldn't go then, so I ate with Ann again and told her about my dinner invitation.

"Your brother's girlfriend, huh?" She smiled. "Stop by the Clinique counter and tell them I sent you. Ask if they have perfume samples you could give to Tracy. It always helps to arrive with something in hand."

"Great idea!" I said. "Thanks!"

Ann took a bite of salad. "So what's she like?"

"Really nice. Smart. She and Lester are both working toward their master's degrees at the U of Maryland."

"Wow! Pretty?"

"Very," I said, and added, "A woman of color."

Ann stopped chewing. "Really? She's black?"

"Yes."

"Hmmm. What do your folks think about this?"

"Dad thinks she's nice. So does Sylvia. She's my stepmom."

Ann appeared to be thinking it over. "Is she Lester's first serious girlfriend?"

I laughed. "*Lester?* He's had a girlfriend ever since I can remember. I couldn't count them all. Two of his girlfriends got married. They were tired of waiting, I guess. But I can tell that Tracy's really special."

"Well, there's no accounting for taste," Ann said. Then, "That didn't come out right. What I meant was, love is a very individual thing."

No, I thought, *she meant what she said the first time.* "I think they're great together," I said.

"Of course," said Ann.

I had a fistful of perfume samples in my bag when I drove home later. I freshened up in the bathroom, put on a little mascara and blush, changed my shirt, and drove over to Lester's.

He lives with two other guys on the second floor of a big Victorian house in Takoma Park. The owner, Otto Watts, has the first floor. The deal is that they get their apartment rent-free as long as one of them is home in the evenings in case old Mr. Watts needs them. And that they do odd jobs around the place. It's a good deal for Les and his buddies and a good deal for Mr. Watts, who has a nursing assistant to care for him during the day.

He was sitting in his wicker rocker on the wrap-around porch when I got out of the car. I waved to him as I headed for the stairway at the side of the house.

"You got lasagna?" he called. He remembered. Liz and Pamela and I had come over once with a surprise supper for Lester, only to find that he had a party going on. So we'd ended up giving it all to Otto.

I laughed. "Not tonight, I'm afraid."

"Make it soon," he said.

At the top of the stairs I knocked, and Les opened the door. "Perfect timing," he said. "We're about ready to eat."

"Hi, Alice!" Tracy called from the kitchen. "Hope you like chicken and sausage over rice."

"Sounds good to me!" I said. She was wearing yellow slacks and a matching sleeveless sweater with a high neck.

"What's this?" she asked as I deposited the perfume samples on the counter.

"Compliments of Hecht's," I told her. "One of my fringe benefits."

"Hey, thanks!" she said.

Lester beamed from the doorway, pleased, I think, that I'd been so thoughtful.

"May I help?" I asked. "Do you want ice in the glasses or anything?"

"That would be wonderful," she said. "And get the butter, would you?"

The small table had been set with a linen cloth and napkins that were decidedly Tracy's. Mostly, I think, Les and George and Paul served their guests buffet-style, sitting wherever they could find a seat.

When I mentioned that to Tracy, she said, "I don't believe in it. I haven't seen a person yet who enjoys balancing a paper plate on his knees."

Lester certainly enjoyed sitting down at a table, I could tell. He'd turned off the game he'd been watching on TV and put on music instead.

"It's delicious, Tracy," I said, a forkful of sausage and rice in my hand.

"Les made the salad," she told me, "but chicken with rice and sausage is an old family recipe. You have old family favorites, don't you?"

I thought of the pineapple upside-down cake I make for Dad. "Sure," I said.

"So who cooks the turkey at your place on Thanksgiving?" she asked.

"Well, most of the time we go out," I said.

"At *Thanksgiving*?" I guessed by the way her eyebrows shot up that we got no points for that.

"Only sometimes," I said quickly. "But Dad always cooks on Christmas Eve."

She smiled then. "That's a great time to have family. Who all comes?"

"To our place? Well . . . Sylvia, of course, now that they're married. And Dad and Les and me."

Tracy actually stopped chewing then. "What about your relatives?"

"Which ones?" I asked.

"Yours! Sylvia's! Don't you have aunts and uncles and cousins?"

"Well . . . yes. One cousin, anyway. No, three, I guess. Sylvia has a niece and nephew. Actually, I've got some older cousins down in Tennessee, but if I ever met them, I don't remember. Our relatives are spread out all over the country. Nobody lives very close."

Tracy looked from me to Lester and back again. "Isn't it lonely?"

I was trying to figure out the correct answer because I wasn't sure if honesty was what was called for here. "Not really," I said. "I mean, I'm used to Les and Dad being family." I didn't have to tell her about Mom dying because she surely knew that by now.

"Well, it's good you feel that way," Tracy said, and started eating again. "I guess I've had so many relatives around that I'm used to a crowd."

"We can arrange one for you," Les said, smiling at her affectionately. "I could always rent a family."

Tracy served bread pudding with rum sauce and raisins for dessert, and I licked up every bite.

"Will you teach me to make this?" I asked.

"Simple as pie," she said.

"Mr. Watts asked if I had any lasagna on me," I told Lester. "He said to bring some the next time I came."

"Could I make up a little dinner for him with these leftovers?" Tracy asked. "He could put it in his fridge for tomorrow."

I could tell from Lester's face that he'd had his eye on those leftovers himself, but he said, "Sure, I'll take them down to him later."

"Let me help with the dishes," I said. "In fact, why don't you two go watch a program or something, and I'll clean up here."

"We always do them together, but three pairs of hands are even better," Les said.

The problem with being the guest of a couple is that you never know just how long you're supposed to stay. If you think they want their privacy and leave right after dinner, it may look as though you came only for the food. But if you hang around after dinner, you wonder if they're waiting for you to go home. I kept watching for a moment alone with Les so I could ask, but it didn't happen. I washed the pots and pans in the sink while Les dried and Tracy put them away.

Then she said, "My aunt gave me a new edition of Trivial Pursuit. Want to play, Alice?"

"Sure," I told her.

So we went into the living room and opened the box. We were using a question pack about history, and I was pleased that I knew so many answers. If Tracy wondered about the IQ of her future sister-in-law, I aced it. The New Deal? I nailed it. Watergate? A cinch.

"You've got a bright sister," Tracy said to Les.

"Well," he said, "sometimes the light's on and sometimes the bulb's a little dim, what can I say?" I gave him a poke.

We talked then about my first two days on the job at Hecht's and about the woman who had stashed all those garments beneath her clothes.

"Sometimes they're repeat offenders, and salespeople know who to look out for," Lester said.

"And sometimes they make mistakes," said Tracy seriously.

"Yeah. That would be embarrassing," I said.

Paul Sorenson came in then, and Tracy got up to get bread pudding for him.

Shall I go? I mouthed to Lester.

Anytime, he mouthed back.

So I followed Tracy out to the kitchen while Les and Paul checked out the baseball game. "It was a great dinner," I told her. "Thanks for the invitation."

"And thanks for the perfume," she said. She gave me a quick hug, one hand holding the dish of pudding. I said good night to Les and Paul and went back out to the car.

Lester seemed so domesticated when he was with Tracy. So content. I thought of buying a T-shirt for Tracy that read I'M THE ONE, but then I thought better of it.

It was a beautiful summer night, perfect for riding with the windows rolled down, my favorite CD in the player. I drove slowly, imagining what it would be like to have my friends in the car, me taking them somewhere. But that wouldn't be for a while. Dad had laid down the law: I couldn't have anyone in the car other than family until I had been driving six months without an accident or a ticket. The slightest fender bender, and the six-month waiting period would begin all over again.

Just then, as though God himself were testing my reflexes, a car on my right came straight through the intersection toward me, even though I had the green light.

I slammed on my brakes and the other driver slammed on his, coming to a stop at a slant, five inches from the hood of Dad's car.

For a moment I thought my heart would rip through my chest, it was pounding so hard. I had the light! I wasn't even speeding! If he hadn't braked, there was nothing I could have done to stop him. And I remembered Dad saying, "You can be right and still be dead, you know." And Les telling me, "Drive as though everyone else is a lunatic."

I was shaking and could feel my hands trembling on the steering wheel. The light had changed now, so I had the red, but I was still out in the middle of the intersection with the other car. Somebody honked. Then someone else. Cars started moving slowly around us. Finally the other driver, a middle-aged man, backed up a little, steered around me, and drove off. Not even a wave. I wondered if I should have got his license plate number. But when the light changed again, I knew just how lucky I had been. I drove home and carefully parked the car in the driveway.

3

Busted

One good thing about not having a boyfriend is that you can be yourself. *More* yourself, anyway. You don't have to worry if he took what you said the wrong way. If he really liked what you gave him for his birthday. If the reason his cell phone was busy all evening was because he was talking to another girl. If he'd be mad if you said you wanted to skip this Saturday—just catch up on stuff you had to do. All those ifs.

But there was a new guy at Mark's pool the following night. Brian brought a friend who wore loud Hawaiian-print trunks. His last name was Keene, and kids called him "Keeno." When Liz said she'd heard he had a dolphin tattoo on his rear end, he promptly lowered his trunks and showed it to us. A fun and crazy kind of guy.

It was a hot night without a breeze, and the water felt great. We lounged around the deck after each swim and dived back into the water whenever the humidity got to us. Keeno and I ended up sharing the same chaise lounge as well as the last slice of pizza the guys had ordered. He grabbed my fingers and licked off a strand of cheese.

"Get *out!*" I laughed. "You're so gross!"

He just grinned. "So how many guys have you gone out with?" he asked.

"Beginning in kindergarten?"

"Sure, if you want."

I'd never really counted before, and suddenly I felt a little embarrassed. Only four boyfriends? Donald Sheavers, Patrick Long, Eric Fielding, and Sam Mayer? Donald Sheavers hardly mattered, and I hadn't gone out with Eric much at all.

"Too many to count," I joked.

"Okay, name the last one." Keeno went to a private school, so he wasn't up on our history.

"Sam Mayer," I said.

"What was he like?"

"Nice. Funny sometimes. Considerate."

"So why'd you dump him? Or were you the dumpee?"

"None of your business!" I told him.

"Okay. Who else?"

"Patrick Long."

"Yeah, I've heard Brian talk about him. The brain,

right? The guy who's going through four years of high school in three?"

"That's Patrick."

"So . . . how far did you go with Patrick?"

This time I pushed him off the chaise lounge. "Get *out*!" I said, glad that Patrick wasn't there to hear all this.

He looked up at me crazily from the deck where he'd landed and seemed perfectly content just to lie there. "If I guess, will you tell me?" he asked.

"No!" I exclaimed, but he made me laugh. Pamela caught on to what he'd been asking, and she laughed too.

"Let's go get some ice cream," someone said.

Most of the kids went inside and changed into jeans or shorts, but Liz and I had walked over to Mark's with cover-ups over our suits and had nothing to change into. I climbed into Brian's car along with Keeno and Mark and Penny, and I hoped my terry-cloth cover-up would absorb the water.

"Baskin-Robbins?" someone called to us from another car.

"No. Let's go to the Creamery," Brian called back, and we were off. It was a longer drive, out past Olney where the land became rural, a nice ride on a summer evening. We rode with the windows down, the breeze drying our hair, a new CD in the player.

When we filed into the Creamery, the manager greeted us like long-lost cousins, happy for our business. Liz and I were giggling because we'd left wet spots on the vinyl seats in Brian's car.

In the Creamery I sat down on a stool at the counter, then moved over one to sit beside Liz.

"Hey! You left the seat wet!" Brian said.

"Don't mind her," Keeno said to the waitress. "Our friend here isn't toilet trained."

"Oh, we're not particular," the waitress joked back, and we laughed as we looked up at the choices listed on the wall and tried to make our selections.

Most of us ordered the double-thick malteds that the Creamery was famous for, but Keeno asked the waitress how much she'd charge to let him make his own.

"I'll have to ask," she said, and went over to talk to the manager. When she came back, she said, "Company rules: You can't go behind the counter, but for two bucks more, you can choose your own ingredients as long as they all fit in the blender."

"Sold!" said Keeno, and we began to smile as he ticked off his choices and the girl at the counter scooped them up: "One scoop each of vanilla, chocolate, and strawberry. . . . One banana . . . butterscotch topping . . . crushed pineapple . . ."

"Keeno, it's going to be gross!" Penny said.

"Uh . . . marshmallow . . . chocolate syrup . . . How much more room we got?"

The waitress showed him the blender. "About an inch more, but you've got to add cream, you know," she said.

"Skip the cream. I want it thick," said Keeno. "Got any blueberries? Peanut butter?"

"Euuw!" said Liz.

When the blender was filled to the top mark, Keeno signaled the waitress. "Start your engines," he said. The blender seemed to groan with the load, and the waitress left it on for three minutes while she and another counter girl filled our orders. When Keeno's shake was finally delivered, it looked more like gravy, and not only his straw, but a metal spoon stuck up straight in the middle of it.

"Mmm! Good!" Keeno said after the first taste, and offered to sell a slurp of it to anyone in the store for a dollar. Of course he got no takers.

It was the kind of evening where everyone was in a good mood. We took our ice cream outside to the patio, where we propped our feet on the metal chairs, listened to the tree frogs, and watched the June bugs and mosquitoes get zapped by the electric insect killer near the door.

Brian was horsing around with Penny. He'd slipped one sandal off and was trying to inch his toes up the calf of her leg. She'd pretend she didn't notice and then, with lightning speed, try to catch his foot in her hand and tickle the bottom.

I could see why guys went for Penny. She wasn't just cute and petite, but she had an infectious laugh—the kind you enjoyed listening to. Sometimes I think guys teased her just to hear her laugh. And I'll have to admit that, except for stealing my boyfriend—okay, *flirting* with him; Patrick did his share—Penny's a nice person, to girls as well as to guys.

Could I ever feel as close to her as I did to Pam and Liz and Gwen? I wondered. I was afraid that if I did, the first thing I'd want to ask her was what it was like with Patrick. Even, how far did they go? I was as bad as Keeno.

But this was an evening to have fun, and back in Brian's car again, Penny and Mark and I squeezed in the backseat, and Penny pointed out that I was still clutching my paper napkin. I joked that I just wanted a souvenir of the evening.

Keeno picked up on that. "You want a souvenir?" he said. "I'll find you a souvenir."

We were the last car in the lineup, and while Brian drove, Keeno kept humming to himself, "Souvenir . . . souvenir . . ." Out beyond the streetlights, trees overhung the dark road. And suddenly Keeno said, "Here! Pull over, Brian," and the car lurched into a small clearing where the two-lane road narrowed down to one lane beside some construction equipment.

Keeno jumped out of the car. Five seconds later he was back, pushing an orange traffic cone ahead of him, over the front seat and onto my lap in back.

"Keeno!" I cried, as we burst into laughter. "What am I supposed to do with this?"

"I don't know," he said. "Put it on your dresser. Hang if from your rearview mirror if you want."

It was one of the smaller cones without the square on the bottom, but still, there was scarcely room for it in the backseat. Every time I tried to move it, it seemed to poke someone, and each time we howled some more.

But the evening wasn't over yet. Penny and Mark wanted a latte at Starbucks. By this time we'd gotten separated from the other cars, so it was only the five of us going for coffee.

We piled out, and I started to leave the traffic cone behind, but Keeno said, "Hey! You wanted a souvenir! You've got to take it with you wherever you go, Alice!"

Everyone shrieked as I stuck it up under my terry-cloth cover-up. At first glance, it looked as though I were pregnant.

You should never try sitting down with a traffic cone under your cover-up. The tip of the cone kept popping out of the neck and poking me under the chin.

"*Bad* baby! Bad! Bad! Bad!" Keeno scolded, shaking his finger at the cone.

I'm sure the other customers thought we were all insane. Penny reached over now and then to stroke my stomach, but I was having a blast. So much fun, in fact, that I forgot the time, and it was ten till midnight when Brian let me out of the car in front of my house. My curfew was eleven thirty.

When I got inside, carrying the traffic cone, Dad was in his armchair, reading the paper in his pajamas.

"The time, Al . . . ," he said, nodding toward the clock on the mantel. Then he saw the traffic cone in my arms and raised one eyebrow.

"It's this new guy, Keeno," I said, laughing. "He's absolutely nuts. He said he'd get me a souvenir of our evening, and before I knew it, he was pushing this traffic cone through the door of Brian's car."

"You drove off with a traffic cone? Where?" asked Dad.

"It's no big deal," I said. "Just some country road repair up beyond Olney."

"Well, you're taking it back," said Dad.

"Oh, *Dad*!"

"You think this is a joke?" he asked. "This could cause an accident, Al!"

"Dad, there were others! It's not like it was the only one!"

"It goes back," said Dad.

"But I don't know exactly where we got it!" I protested.

"Then you'll call up this boy and find out," Dad insisted.

I imagined myself having to call Brian and get Keeno's number. Then telling Keeno that we had to take it back.

"Well, maybe I can find the place myself," I said quickly.

I honestly didn't think he'd hold me to it. But at a quarter of eight the next morning Dad tapped on my bedroom door and said, "What time are you due at Hecht's today?"

I could barely open one eye. "Noon," I murmured.

"Well, I need to be at my store by nine, so get dressed. We're going to return that traffic cone," he said.

"Dad!" I protested sleepily.

"I want you dressed and in the car in fifteen minutes," he told me.

I sat sullenly in the front seat, the stupid traffic cone on my lap, and tried to direct Dad to the route we'd taken home from the Creamery the night before.

After a couple of turns I figured out the site was on a northern road off Georgia Avenue, and sure enough, we saw the construction crew and a line of traffic cones, minus one, narrowing the two lanes to one.

Dad pulled off onto the shoulder as the men on the crew looked up. I could feel my cheeks burn as I opened the car door. Holding the cone in front of me, I walked over to the others and placed mine at the end of the row. Then I quickly got back in the car.

They were staring at me—five men in sleeveless T-shirts, tattoos the length of their arms.

One of them gave Dad a sort of play salute. Dad turned back on the road again, and we drove for a while without speaking. If Dad made a big scene over a little thing like a traffic cone, I thought, what would he do when something big happened?

"I could have come home drunk or pregnant, you know," I said, glaring.

"That's supposed to make me feel better?" he said. "A family could have failed to notice that the road narrowed until a second too late and been killed, Al."

He always paints the most extreme thing that could possibly happen.

I was quiet some more. Finally I said, "Weren't *you* ever sixteen once?"

"Yes, and that's why I'm being extra cautious with you," he said. "If you want to convince me you're a responsible driver, show me you're responsible even when you're not driving."

Then I shut up because I had five more months to go before he'd let me have friends in the car when I drove, and it would be his car I was driving. *If* I was driving.

I wondered what Patrick would have said if he'd been in the car with us last night. Patrick is so darn responsible sometimes that he seems like a grown man already.

I saw him later that week at the CVS drugstore. You never want to run into a guy friend at the drugstore because you could be buying something embarrassing. Fortunately, I had only a package of Gillette Venus razors in my hand. Patrick was picking up some batteries.

"Did Mark tell you the gang is trying to get together every Monday night at his pool?" I asked.

"Yeah, I heard, but I had something else on Monday," Patrick said. His smile was as friendly as ever, but somehow I felt that the "something" was probably "someone," and the someone was probably Marcie, the girl he'd taken to the Jack of Hearts dance last spring.

"So how's it going?" I asked, meaning Marcie.

"Life's good," said Patrick, meaning everything, I guess.

"Gearing up for your senior year?"

"Yeah. We start doing the old college tour this fall," he said.

"Where do you want to go?"

"I'm applying at the University of Chicago and Bennington, for sure. After that, I don't know."

Illinois and Vermont, I thought. They seemed so far away. The guy I'd known since sixth grade would be a "college man" while I was still back in Maryland borrowing traffic cones. I suddenly felt very insignificant and silly.

"Well," I said, "I hope you can make it over to Mark's one of these Mondays. We missed you."

"Really?" There was a twinkle in his eye. "You too?"

I felt the slight reddening of my cheeks again. "We all did," I said quickly, and he just grinned.

"I'll go over one of these nights," he said, and gave me a little tap on the elbow. "See ya."

"See ya," I repeated as he ambled on through the store.

I guess I still had feelings for Patrick—now and

then, anyway. I wondered how I compared to Marcie.

Well, I told myself as I left the store, *we can't all be brains.* And I *did* have a good time on Monday night with Keeno. But I was also glad that Patrick *hadn't* been there, *hadn't* been in the car, *hadn't* had to sit beside that traffic cone all the way back to my house.

4

Extreme Mortification

The following Saturday we were having an early-bird sale at Hecht's. I had to be at the store at seven forty-five and was off at four. Liz and Gwen met me after work, and we went down to sit with Pamela during her dinner break outside Burger King.

"One thing's certain," said Pamela. "I don't want to toss burgers for the rest of my life. My hands, my clothes—even my hair—all smell like hamburger grease when I get home."

"And I don't want to have more than three children," Liz said, sipping her Coke. "I love the little kids at day camp, but I don't like six or seven of them all clamoring for me at the same time."

I already knew that *I* didn't want to work with clothes for the rest of my life, so I said, "How's it going at NIH, Gwen? What department is it again?"

"Hematology," said Gwen.

"Translation?" said Pamela.

"Study of blood. Blood disorders," Gwen told us.

"Now, *that* ought to put you in the mood for dinner," Liz said.

"Oh, everything I work with is in tubes and bottles," Gwen said. "If I go into medicine, though, I think I'd like to work with patients, not research."

"I wish we had a crystal ball and could see what each of us would be doing ten years from now," said Liz.

"You? Married, three kids," said Pamela.

"I wish," Liz said.

"I'll bet I know who *will* be married ten years from now. *Five* years, even, if she can arrange it," said Pamela. "Jill. To Justin. She was telling me the other night that his dad made millions in real estate."

"And so it naturally follows that . . . ?" I said.

"That she'd be marrying into money," said Pamela.

"But she flirts with everything in pants!" I said.

Pamela gave a little laugh. "Jill's got a wandering eye, but she's got 'million-dollar wedding' dreams. She wants to fly all her guests to the Bahamas."

"Spare me," said Gwen.

A few years back Justin was new to our group, and he and Liz were a couple for a while. But the romance cooled, and Jill took over. If any girl in our group is a "babe," it's Jill. And if any babe ever wanted to be the center of attention, this is the one.

"Do you ever get the feeling that for a lot of brides the wedding's more important than the groom?" I asked.

"Depends on the groom," said Pamela.

After Pamela went back to work, Liz and Gwen and I returned to Hecht's to do some shopping. Gwen was looking for a watch with a bold second hand and timer, and Liz needed a new wallet. I was trying on sunglasses, and for a while we were each at different counters.

I had just put on a pair with green-tinted lenses when I noticed a familiar-looking man in a light Windbreaker fingering the gold chains in the jewelry section. Then he moved on over to earrings. I finally recognized him as the store detective, playing at being a customer, and then I realized something else: He was following Gwen.

I put down the shades I was holding. From where I stood, it appeared that Gwen had taken two watches out of their boxes on the display rack and was checking them over. The store detective moved from earrings to a second table of watches, where he could see Gwen a little better. Was I the only one who realized that a man who goes around a store in a light Windbreaker, summer and winter, with a walkie-talkie on his belt beneath his jacket, has got to be a store detective?

Whenever Gwen looked up, the detective looked down—picked up a watch himself and looked it over. What did he think—that Gwen was going to stick one in her bag? Slip it in her bra?

At last Gwen put one watch down, folded up the instruction sheet she'd been reading, tucked it back in the carton, and carried the other watch over to the cashier. At that point the detective lost interest and headed for another department.

"Did you find anything interesting?" Liz asked me when she came over with the wallet she was going to buy.

I wasn't supposed to point out security personnel, I knew. So I just said, "Yeah. Really interesting, but I don't want to buy anything yet."

I didn't tell Gwen she'd been under surveil-lance. Somehow I figured she was used to it by now. What was it like, I wondered, to know that you were a prime suspect every time you entered a store? That if one out of every five customers was going to be tailed, you were that one? How did it feel to know that your grades, your family, your church—all the things that were important to you—didn't make a bit of difference when you went shopping; that the thing they could see—the color of your skin—was the determining factor?

"Find what you wanted?" I asked as she came toward us carrying her purchase.

"Sort of," she said. She glanced toward the store detective, who was now staking out someone else. "And about what I expected," she added.

I'd heard people say that they almost died of embarrassment or that they wished the ground would open and swallow them up. I'd felt that many more times than I could count, but somehow I thought I was outgrowing it—that the really embarrassing things happen only to middle school kids. And then . . . there was Thursday. I don't see how it could have been worse.

Both Dad and Sylvia needed their cars, so I had to take a bus directly from work to my orthodontist, and then another bus back home. The whole afternoon was a bummer. Getting my braces tightened always gives me a headache anyway. The soreness in my mouth radiates up into my cheekbones, and then my head starts to throb. The family scatters when I come home from the orthodontist, I've noticed, and I can't say I blame them.

I was wearing a sheer rayon blouse with short flutter sleeves, a white cotton skirt, and sneakers. I know how to dress for work now—cool top and comfortable shoes. And a skirt is cooler than pants. On this particular day I'd been working in the juniors department, picking up after eleven- and twelve-year-old girls who were trying on bathing suits.

They'd descend on the fitting rooms in groups of four or five, and while one girl went inside a cubicle and locked the door, the others would crowd around outside calling out encouragement and instructions.

"Tighten the ties on the sides, Mary Ann."

"Maybe you need two different sizes for top and bottom."

"You might need a bikini wax, Hannah."

"Don't look in the mirror till you've got the top on."

Then the moment of truth, when their friend unlocked the door. They'd all crowd in, shrieking and exclaiming.

"Were we ever like that?" I asked the saleswoman out at the cash register.

"What do you mean, 'were'?" she said. "I still drag a friend with me when I shop for a swimsuit."

It was like leaving an aviary when I caught the bus later—all that chatter and screeching and cawing. I think I had a headache before I even sat down at the orthodontist's; I was feeling lousy anyway, and his fingers in my mouth didn't help.

Just before he got to the last section of wire, I realized what was happening. I was having my period four days early.

My white skirt!

"Uhggghhhh," I said with a jolt.

"That hurt?" he asked. "One more minute here and I'm done."

I closed my eyes, but my eyeballs bulged behind the lids. What was I going to *do*? Stupidly, I didn't have anything with me.

Another gush between my legs. A feeling of warmth. Some periods start out heavy like this from the very first day. *This can't be happening!* I thought. I could feel the sweat on my palms against the leather armrests.

"Okay . . . about . . . one second more. . . . Done!" the orthodontist said, backing away. "Looking good, Alice. Call in for your next appointment, will you? There's nobody at the desk right now. Cheryl's sick today, and Joan's doing double duty from back here." In the next cubicle his assistant was putting an X-ray on the screen.

I got out of the chair, feeling sticky and moist. Trying to keep my thighs together, I made it to the small restroom in the hallway and locked the door behind me. Lifting my skirt, I found a red spot the size of Texas in my panties.

I stuffed myself with toilet paper and tried to soak up the blood on my underwear with paper towels. Then I grabbed the waistband of my skirt and slid it round to the front. A bright red spot decorated the back.

The chair! I thought. The orthodontist's chair! I'd probably bled on that! I thought maybe I could take a paper towel and sneak back in there before the next patient sat down in it.

Pulling off my skirt, I ran the spot under cold water. A stream of pink swirled around in the sink bowl. *Stupid, stupid, stupid!* I told myself. How could I have left home without some tampons or pads in my bag?

Someone rattled the door handle.

"Somebody's in there!" I heard a child complain.

Then Joan's, the assistant's, voice: "I'm sure she'll be out in a minute."

And the kid's voice: "Mom, I really have to *go!*"

Why couldn't there be an escape button I could press, so that a trapdoor would open beneath me and I could just slide through? I wondered.

I shut off the faucet and tried to press the worst of the water and stain off my skirt. Now it was a huge wet *pink* spot instead—the size of the United States—and it looked as though I'd wet my pants.

"Hey!" the kid said, rattling the door handle again. "Is anybody in there?"

"Just a minute," I called.

I put my skirt on again and, with a couple of paper towels inside my pants, opened the door to face a boy in a baseball cap glaring at me.

"Hurry *up*!" he said, pushing past me, and I made up my mind right then that I wouldn't even try to wipe off the chair for him. Let him explain *that* to his mom when she did the laundry.

I went out to the lobby of the building, took out my cell phone, and dialed home. No answer, of course. Sylvia was teaching summer school three days a week. I knew that Liz and Gwen and Pamela were all at work, and Les had a course on Thursdays. Dad? Reluctantly, I called the Melody Inn.

"He's not here right now," David told me. "He and Marilyn are next door looking over the space. We're thinking of adding an annex, you know."

I wasn't interested in an annex at the moment; I was interested in Kotex. I walked outside, but there was no drugstore in sight and I didn't have enough money for a cab. It had to be the bus.

I could see one coming two blocks away and got out my change. Another girl was waiting too, and

I could see her staring at my skirt. I kept my eyes straight ahead. A woman came hurrying down the sidewalk to board the bus. As I got on and moved down the aisle to a seat, she whispered behind me, "Use bleach, sweetheart. It'll get the stain out."

I thought I was home free at this point, but when I sat down, the paper towels shifted to one side and I could feel the blood trickling out. I'd had dreams like this, and I always woke up at the worst moment. But now I couldn't stop the Niagara Falls inside my pants, and it wasn't a dream. When we reached my stop, I had to walk to the front of the bus in full view of all the passengers. I knew what was on the back of my skirt now without even looking.

I didn't look to the left or the right. *I am woman!* I told myself as the door swung open. *I am woman!* I said again as I passed some girls playing hopscotch on the sidewalk, their giggling, taunting voices following me when they noticed my skirt.

At home Lester's car was parked in our driveway, but I didn't even stop to talk to him when I got inside. I rushed on upstairs to change my clothes. When I came down again, he was sitting in the kitchen, eating an English muffin.

"I thought you had a class today," I said accusingly.

"I did! It's over! Am I committing a crime or

something?" he asked. "Hey, it's only an English muffin."

"Never mind," I told him, and took my bloody clothes to the basement. Why couldn't I have had a sister? I wondered. A lot of sisters, in fact, to commiserate with me as soon as I walked in the door? Guys don't know how good they have it. It's not enough that we menstruate five days a month. We don't even know for sure when those five days are going to be! *Do I have to spend the rest of my life wearing Kotex?* I asked myself. *Do I have to cram tampons in my pencil case to be safe? Do I have to keep pads tucked away in my backpack, my gym shoes, my locker?*

I threw my clothes into the washing machine and took a Tylenol. *Is there anything else that could possibly happen to me worse than this?* I wondered. *What if this had happened at school? What if it had happened when I went out with someone? At a dance? At the pool?* Did I always have to live as though any minute I could have another Most Embarrassing Moment of My Life?

And I guess the answer was yes.

A half hour later I had set the table for dinner and was waiting for Sylvia when the phone rang.

It was Gwen. I was about to launch into my account of the Texas-size spot on the back of my skirt when she said, "Molly said I could tell you. I saw her in a lab at work today."

"Molly's working at NIH?" I said, suddenly envious that *two* of my friends had internships there this summer.

"No, she's a patient," Gwen said. "Acute lymphoblastic leukemia."

"Oh . . . Gwen!" I said, catching my breath.

"Isn't this awful?" she said. "We're not supposed to give out information about patients, but she said I should tell you and Liz and Pamela."

I thought about the school trip we'd taken to New York this past spring. Remembered suddenly the paleness of her face that day at Ellis Island. The way she went to bed early the evening the rest of us sneaked out for a night on the town. The times she remarked how tired she was.

Molly—the hardworking, blue-eyed girl on stage crew, everybody's friend. We never dreamed . . .

"Oh, Gwen!" I said again. "How bad is it?"

"I asked the doctors. They said it's possible that after treatment she'll go into remission and then have a relapse, but they're hoping for a cure. There's a high cure rate for this type of cancer, but of course, they just don't know. Usually it's younger kids who get this."

"Can she have visitors? Does she *want* us to come and see her?"

"She'll be here a few days for more tests. They've entered her in a twelve-month protocol—a study. There's a lot of research going on about leukemia." I heard Gwen sigh. "It *would* have to be Molly, wouldn't it? The girl everybody loves. Will you let Pam and Liz know? I'll call Faith. Molly wanted me to tell her, too."

I didn't want to call anyone for a while. I went up to my room and sat down by the window, staring at the sky. If I could walk out of the orthodontist's a hundred times—a thousand, even—with blood on the back of my skirt, I'd do it in a second for Molly. But you don't get to bargain when it comes to illness. I picked up the phone and called Liz.

5

Facing Up

It was as though my mom were dying all over again, and this time I'd have to deal with it. Mom had leukemia too, but I'd been too young to know what it was. What it meant. I didn't know she wasn't coming back and I'd never see her again.

"You said that Gwen told you they're hoping for a cure," Liz reminded me after we'd talked awhile.

"I know," I said, trying to keep my tears in check. "But it shouldn't have happened to Molly. Nothing bad should happen to Molly."

"Life is so fucking unfair," Liz said. When Elizabeth says the *F* word, you *know* she's upset.

When I called Pamela and told her, she said, "We've got to do something nice for her, Alice! We've got to make her senior year really great."

"How are we going to do that?" I asked. "We don't even know if she'll be coming back in September."

"Get her a boyfriend," said Pamela.

With Pamela, there are few things in life that can't be fixed by a boyfriend. "You're kidding, of course," I said.

"On the contrary. I think it's one of the best ideas I ever had. She needs someone to call her, take her out, hug her, excite her. . . ."

"Pamela," I said, "have you ever been really, really sick?"

"I had my tonsils out," said Pamela.

"Molly didn't need a boyfriend when she was well, so now she needs one as a crutch? Is that it?"

"It couldn't hurt."

I sat for a long time with the phone in my lap and thought about Molly. It was years after Mom died that I even got up the nerve to ask Dad what she had died of. And we'd never had "the talk." I'd never really asked for details. It was just too scary, as though, if I asked, the floodgates would open. I'd start crying and never be able to stop. As though, if I learned too much about leukemia, it would suddenly start growing in *my* body. Like *cancer* and *leukemia* were voodoo words, and as long as you didn't say them, they'd keep their distance.

Les stayed for dinner, and I told everyone about Molly. But I didn't want to ask about Mom just

then. I waited till Lester had gone home and Sylvia
and I had cleaned up the dishes. Then I went out
to sit on the back porch beside Dad, who was still
enjoying his coffee.

"What I'd like to do," he said as I took the chair
across from him, stretching out my legs and resting my toes on the edge of his seat, "is put on a
new porch, twice as big, and screen it in. Would
be a nice place to eat dinner and spend a summer
evening. Catch a breeze."

"Sounds great," I said. "I could even have a
sleepover on it. Or just hang out with my friends."

"We could use it for a lot of things," said Dad.
"That's one thing Marie and I always wanted and
never got. A screened porch."

I was glad he'd given me an opening.

"Dad . . ." I hesitated. "What was it like? *Really*
like, I mean, when Mom got sick?"

He went on staring out over the backyard.
"Awful," he said.

I waited. "I was so little," I said finally. "I just
didn't know what all you and Les were going
through. I remember seeing Lester cry, though."

"We were worried for you, too, honey."

"That I'd get leukemia?"

"No. About how confusing it must have been
for you and how much you missed your mother."

"I had Aunt Sally."

"Yes, bless her. What would any of us have done without her and your uncle Milt?"

"Was Mom sick for a long time?" I asked.

"No. She went pretty fast."

"Was hers worse than what Molly's got, then?"

"Yes. It was a different kind. There was no talk of a cure when Marie got sick."

"How did she know she had it?"

"We both knew she was tired a lot, but that could have been due to a lot of things. The first symptom she told me about was the bleeding. Her nose . . . her gums . . . and finally every opening of her body. She died three and a half months later. That's how quick she went."

"What was *she* like? I mean, how did she take it?"

"She was scared. She was just very scared. We both were. Then, after the shock of it, she worried about you and Lester. I knew that my job from then on was to reassure her that I would raise you two okay."

"And you have, Dad," I said quickly.

He gave my toes a little pinch. "So far," he said, with a warning smile. Then he added, "I guess she saw *her* job as being brave. I don't think either of us was very good at it, but we did the best we could." He sat very still then, one hand covering my toes like a protective umbrella.

"Would it have been better or worse if she'd lived longer?" I asked.

"Sick, you mean? Probably worse. As it was, she didn't have long periods where she just felt okay. Each day she was weaker; she was always bleeding from somewhere." I saw Dad's chin tremble a little. "She died . . . with me stroking her hair. That's one good thing I have to hold on to . . . that I was beside her, stroking her hair." He pulled out a handkerchief and blew his nose.

I looked away. "I think I remember going to see her once. Did I visit her in the hospital?"

"Yes. They wheeled her down to the 'sunroom,' they called it. I brought you in, and you were frightened at first because of the IV hookup—all the tubes. But then I sat you on her lap—"

"I remember that! And I remember that she smelled different. I didn't think it was her at first because her legs were so bony." I could feel tears welling up in my own eyes. "Then she put her lips against my ear and hummed my favorite song, and I knew it was her. And we snuggled. . . ." I swallowed. "And I cried when I had to leave."

"So did she, Al. And so did I."

I decided to invite Les and Tracy for dinner that weekend and to cook the meal myself. Sylvia had taught me how to broil fish—simple as anything—so I planned my menu and set the table for five.

I peeled the potatoes and boiled them with tiny onions. Steamed some cauliflower, and after rinsing off the trout fillets, I dotted them with bits of butter and spread them out on a big broiler pan. Then I salted them lightly, sprinkled them with lemon juice, and added a dash of dill weed from the spice drawer.

About four minutes later, when the fillets were just starting to turn golden on top, I took them from the oven and called everyone to the table.

It's a wonderful feeling when you cook something that tastes just the way it's supposed to— the way it would taste if Sylvia had made it herself. The only thing I hadn't made were the club rolls, and I passed those around in a basket.

"Pretty good, Al," said Dad.

Just *pretty* good? I thought the meal was terrific.

"It's wonderful," said Sylvia. "The seasoning is just right."

"Rainbow trout is one of my favorites," said Tracy.

Lester was the only one who didn't say anything. If you want the truth, go to Lester. "Is there a problem?" I asked.

"I'm not sure," said Les, holding up a piece of

cauliflower on his fork. "Is it just me, or is everything on my plate the same color?"

It suddenly hit me: It *was*! I don't think I'd ever
thought about color in a meal. I mean, as long as
it tasted good . . .

"It's still delicious," said Sylvia. "Next time you
might just add a salad or some green beans."

"A few slices of red tomato," said Tracy.

"An ear of yellow corn would be nice," said Dad.

Of course! How could I not have realized that an
appetizing meal can't be all one color? And then I
had an awful thought: Would Tracy think I was
making a statement? That I didn't want any other
color at our table?

I was miserable for the rest of the meal. *Anguished*
at the thought of my homemade coconut cake in
the kitchen still waiting to be served. With vanilla
ice cream yet! When Tracy helped me carry the
plates back to the kitchen, I stammered, "I r-really
wasn't trying to make a statement, Tracy! I just
didn't think!"

"What?" she said.

"About the cauliflower and the potatoes."

"What?" she said. "I like cauliflower and potatoes."

"Everything on the menu was *white*!" I wailed.

Tracy burst out laughing. "Les was right about
you," she said.

"What about me?"

"He said if you didn't have enough to worry about, you'd make something up. I don't make it my occupation to go around looking for ways people are politically incorrect, Alice. Life is too short, too personal, and far too spontaneous for that."

"Whew! I'm glad."

She grinned at me as she studied the coconut cake on the counter. The cake I'd spent the evening before baking and frosting. "And I'm sure not going to argue with you over *that* gorgeous thing," she said. "But I tell you what. Anytime you want to serve a *dark* meal, make it caviar and chocolate pie, and I'll think I've died and gone to heaven."

Keeno was at Mark's again when we met for our Monday-night swim. He was wearing a new pair of floral trunks that had red and yellow parrots on them. They also looked a size too big, and each time he climbed out of the water, they almost fell off.

Brian had definitely been smoking weed before we got there—I've learned to recognize the odor now after someone pointed it out to me in the school parking lot. Whether Keeno or Mark smoked it too, I wasn't sure, but I'd be surprised if the Stedmeisters knew about it. Brian carried a little bottle of Visine around in his pocket and joked about his red eyes once—said he'd gotten wasted the night before. But we knew better. One way or the other, of course, he was right.

Everyone showed up this particular Monday, even Patrick. *Without* a girl in tow, I might add. Jill and Justin were there, looking like a married couple. Justin carried all of Jill's stuff, and they had those private little glances and signals and code words that excluded everyone else. We were used to that.

We all chipped in and ordered pizza, and after it was delivered, we got into this really weird discussion about a girl at Georgetown University who claimed she was date-raped. We were wondering how you would ever prove that it wasn't consensual.

"I'll bet ninety percent of the girls claiming date rape brought it on themselves," Brian muttered. He settled back in the deck chair with his hands over his stomach, eyes half-closed. Reminded me of that old movie, *The Godfather.*

"*Excuse* me?" I said.

"*You* know," Brian continued. "They get the guys all hotted up, and when he can't hold back any longer, they cry rape."

"Can't hold back any longer?" Gwen said

incredulously. "What are we talking about here? The Hoover Dam?"

"I used to go with a guy who thought he was an uncontrollable force and I was an immovable object," said Gwen's friend Yolanda, who had started hanging out with us. "To listen to him, if he didn't get what he wanted, he'd erupt or something."

Karen is Jill's best friend, and, like Jill, she usually agrees with the guys. But this time she said, "I don't care *what* signals a girl's giving or a guy *thinks* she's giving—if a girl says no, she means it."

"Not!" said Mark. "Not always. Sometimes she just likes to tease a little first. Makes for better sex." Oh, yeah. Mark Stedmeister, Man of Experience. Right.

"So you're saying that sometimes it's okay to force yourself on someone?" I asked.

"I wouldn't say 'force,' exactly," put in Keeno.

"If a girl's been giving a guy the go-ahead all evening and then backs off, I think he has a right to figure she really wants it," said Mark.

"Or if a guy spends a bundle on her and she doesn't put out, he's entitled to a little something," said Brian.

"I don't *believe* this!" I said.

"Okay, what if he's *married* to her?" said Mark.

"What if they're married and she says no? Sex is part of marriage, right? So he's entitled to take a little." He turned to Patrick, who was finishing a slice of pizza. "Right?"

Patrick shrugged and took a drink of his Sprite. "Why would he want to?"

Keeno leered around the group. "Why would he want *sex*?"

"No. Wouldn't he want her to . . . you know . . . enjoy it too?" said Patrick.

It was like I was back in the Our Whole Lives class at church. "*Thank* you, Patrick," I said. "At least there's one sane male around here." I could have gone over and kissed him, anchovies and all. He sounded so mature, like he was in college already!

But Brian and Keeno and Mark kept at it. "If she's resisting, makes it all the better!" Brian said.

Justin agreed with Patrick, though, and Jill gazed at him adoringly and slid his hand between her knees. I saw Gwen make a gagging gesture, my cue to slide into the pool. Several of us swam to the deep end as the talk disintegrated into which couples from school were "getting any" and which weren't.

Mark's pool has a light at the bottom so that anyone swimming at the top is just a silhouette. If you put your face under, you could make out a coin or a pebble, it's so bright down there. It's fun to watch the swimmers if you're sitting out on the deck. More fun to be one of them.

I swam around with Gwen and Yolanda, and when we stopped to tread water, Gwen said, "If all the male chauvinists in our school were laid end to end—"

"—they'd be happy!" Yolanda finished without missing a beat, and we laughed there beneath the diving board and wouldn't let the guys in on the joke.

Gwen and Liz and Pamela and I went to see Molly. Faith had called us to say she'd pick us up in her mom's car. Liz and I squeezed into the backseat beside Pamela, Gwen up front.

I'd half expected to see Ron, Faith's scumbag ex-boyfriend, in the car, but Faith was alone. When she saw the relief on my face, she said, "Relax. Ron's history." It was the best thing I'd heard in weeks.

"How's Molly's morale?" Liz asked her. Faith had graduated last spring, and Molly was a senior now, so they knew each other better than we knew Molly.

"What can I say?" Faith said. "How can she do anything but just tough it out?"

We were quiet for a minute, and I thought of all

the work Molly had put into stage crew last spring.

"Only four months ago, we were working together on *Father of the Bride*," I said. "She seemed okay, but she might have been feeling rotten even then."

"All those long rehearsals, and she kept the rest of us going," said Pamela.

"Well, now it's our turn," said Faith. "We've got to make sure that at least one of us comes by to see her once a week. Maybe we could work out a schedule."

Molly's mom met us at the door. "How nice of you!" she said when she saw us. "Molly's in the living room. Go right in."

Molly was in a sweat suit at one end of the couch, propped up on pillows and reading *People* magazine. Her face lit up when she saw us.

"Well . . . hey!" she said, dropping the magazine on the floor and scooting up into a sitting position. "Sit down, guys!"

"Your friendly neighborhood get-well wagon," Faith said. She leaned down and gave Molly a hug. "How you doing?"

"Haven't the faintest. Only the blood tests know. But it's great to see you," Molly said.

What do you say to somebody who may or may not die a lot sooner than she'd expected?

What do you say to someone who feels like crap—that no matter what's going on in your life, hers is worse?

"We've all been waiting to come over," I told her. "We're glad you're home."

"Yeah. So am I," said Molly. "I can't say I feel any better at home, but the amenities are nicer."

"When do you start chemo?" Gwen asked her.

"Next week, I think," said Molly. "You probably know more about me than I do, Gwen."

"Nothing you don't know already," Gwen assured her.

"So how are you spending the summer?" asked Liz.

Molly motioned to a stack of books on the end table. "AP English," she said. "I don't know how much school I'll miss, so I'm trying to do some of the work now." She grinned sheepishly down at the magazine on the floor. "Recess," she said, pointing, and we laughed.

"What do you have to do for AP English?" I asked. "I may be up for that." I wasn't entirely sure I would *qualify* for advanced placement anything, but it couldn't hurt to try.

"An analysis of Dante's *Inferno*, a three-thousand-word essay on *Interpretations of Myths and Meanings in Beowulf*, and a four-page essay on *Revisiting The Grapes of Wrath*."

"Oh, wow!" said Pamela.

Molly's mom brought in some iced tea, and after she left, Molly started talking about how weird it was to be thinking about your senior year on stage crew, the debate team, the Latin Club, the prom . . . and then, after a day at the doctor's, to suddenly see the whole year from your living room couch.

I think we decided by the end of that afternoon that she didn't want us to tell her how we knew she'd get better; she didn't want to hear that a cousin or neighbor had the same disease and made medical history by drinking gallons of vitamin C. She didn't want us to cry or give her the name of our doctor or listen to our idea of what made her sick in the first place. She didn't want us to find her a boyfriend.

All Molly wanted was for us to listen. And the only helpful response, when she said what a dirty deal it was that she'd be sick her senior year, was, "Yes, it is, Molly. It really sucks."

6

Planning

"I think Dad may be getting married again," Pamela told me.

"Really? Have you met her?" I asked.

"Yeah. It's the nurse. They've been on-again, off-again, but I went out to dinner with them the other night, and they were definitely on-again. Why else would they take me out to dinner with them unless they wanted me to know they were serious?"

We'd managed to take a break at the same time that afternoon—me from Hecht's and Pamela from Burger King.

"What's she like?" I asked.

Pamela shrugged. "Nice, I guess. Sort of plain compared to Mom. I wouldn't call her sexy, exactly, but . . . Hey, what do I know? Maybe Dad's had enough of 'sexy.'"

"Does your mom know about her?"

"Are you kidding? *I'm* not going to tell her, that's for sure. She says she's over him now, but don't you believe it." We crumpled up our sandwich wrappers and took them to the trash. "What department are you working today?" Pamela asked.

"Infants and toddlers," I said. "I'm stocking sleepers, overalls, socks, booties. . . . Did you know you could buy a shirt and top for yourself with what it costs to outfit a toddler?"

"If I ever have kids, they'll run around naked," Pamela joked.

When I got back to the store, they sent me to the employees' lounge with a group for training on shoplifting. A Montgomery County police officer was showing a film on how to spot thieves, and Sergeant Camfield—a sturdy brunette with plucked eyebrows—showed us some shoplifters' accessories, from baggy trousers to large jackets with big inside pockets to shopping bags lined with foil to keep the plastic sensors from tripping the security detectors.

"Booster bags," she called them, showing how one thief had covered the foil with duct tape to disguise it and had also fashioned firm handles by cutting out hand holes in the plastic and wrapping the edges with tape. We don't put security sensors on all our stuff, just the things shoplifters are most likely to want.

"Don't ever confront a thief yourself," Jennifer Martin, from the personnel office, said. "If you see someone with merchandise in hand, you might say, 'May I ring that up for you?' or 'Do you want me to hold this for you at the counter while you look around some more?' But if you see someone in the act of shoplifting, call the security number." And she told us what that number was and what the code word was for the week.

"Learn to look for the unexpected," Sergeant Camfield said. "If we have to give shoplifters credit for anything, it's originality. Sometimes it's the shopper you'd least expect."

When I got back to my department, the head clerk asked, "Well, did you learn anything?"

"Yeah," I said. "Look for toddlers in overcoats and baggy diapers," and she laughed.

All anyone wanted to talk about, though, was vacation—when they were going or where they had been.

"You going anywhere this summer?" the clerk asked me later as we stacked packages of infant undershirts on a sale table.

"I don't think so," I told her. "What about you?"

"I've been here a year, so I get a week," she said. "West Virginia, maybe. They say you're either a beach person or a mountain person, and I never did like the water."

I'd take whatever I could get, I decided. July turned into August, each day hotter than the one before. Dad let me use the car to drive over to Molly's and critique some of the stuff she'd written for her essays. See if it was clear. I was glad to do it, but I couldn't exactly call it a vacation.

I was feeling sorry for myself because I didn't have any plans for a trip. Dad and Sylvia were saving money for remodeling our house. The most I could expect was a night at the movies. Then I thought of Molly. The most she could expect was to write some acceptable essays in the month we had left, and I felt ashamed of myself.

Jennifer Martin put me in misses' sportswear for the rest of the summer. She said they'd be having almost continuous sales until the last of the summer stock was gone.

Juanita was the department manager of sportswear. She was about forty, short, and had long shiny hair, almost blue-black. She said that whenever the fitting rooms were clear, I could help out on the floor directing customers toward their favorite brands and finding the right size for customers in the fitting rooms.

Now that I could move around the floor more, friends came by to say hello. It added a little novelty to my day, but it also caused problems. We're not supposed to visit with friends on the job, but if they want to buy something, it's okay. When Penny came by looking for petites, I showed her some fabulous gauze tops to wear with jeans.

"These are great!" she said. "But aren't you working at your dad's store this summer?"

I rolled my eyes. "He wants me to broaden my horizons, explore the world."

"Here in the sportswear department?" she said, and we laughed. "Good luck."

It was Karen and Jill who gave me trouble. When Karen came by a few days later and picked out a swimsuit and cover-up, she waited till I'd gone back to the fitting rooms, then cornered me there. "Alice, how about letting me use your employee discount? I'm paying cash, so who's to know?"

"I'm not sure, Karen," I said reluctantly.

"What's the harm? It could have been you paying cash, right? Some stores even have a 'family and friends' discount."

"Well . . . just this once," I said.

I wasn't allowed to ring up sales, though, so Karen gave me the money and wandered off while I waited for a break in customers. Then I asked Juanita to ring them up for me, employee discount.

"Boy, you can buy a bathing suit just like that?" she said. "Did you even try this on?"

"It'll fit," I said, and gave her my employee number.

And then, wouldn't you know, Jill came in the next day.

"Omigod!" she said. "I can't believe it! I found these jeans in my size—for tall girls, you know? I've looked all over for them."

"Your lucky day," I said. They were great-looking jeans and cost more than I'd ever pay. Jill followed me over to a rack where I was marking down summer jackets and said, "Alice, please, *please* let me use your employee discount."

"Oh, Jill, I can't," I said. "I'm going to be in big trouble if they catch me."

"Are you kidding? Everyone does it!" she said. "They *expect* you to do it! I haven't been able to find these anywhere else, and they're *so* expensive. And you know what long legs I've got. . . ."

"Look. Just this once," I said. "Do you have the money?"

"Yeah. Barely."

"Come back in a half hour," I told her, and she disappeared among the shoppers.

I took the jeans over to Juanita later and asked her to ring them up for me.

"Aren't these a little long for you, Alice?" she asked. "In fact, they'd be *much* too long."

"A gift for my cousin," I lied. "She's got legs to

die for." I could tell by the look she gave me that she didn't quite believe me.

I wasn't exactly cheerful when Jill came back. "The line stops here," I said. "Don't even think of telling anyone else, because I can't do it again."

"You're a sweetheart," Jill said, and walked away on her extra-long legs.

One girl who didn't ask for a discount made trouble of a different sort.

"Hey, Alice, I didn't know you worked here!" a voice said one afternoon, and I turned to see Amy Sheldon from school. Some of the girls call her "Amy Clueless" because she never quite seems to be "with it." She's a master at non sequiturs, and she doesn't appear to know how she affects other people. Even though you want to be kind to people with disabilities—if that's what it was with Amy—it doesn't mean they can't drive you nuts sometimes.

"Hi, Amy," I said. "Yeah, they keep me busy, all right." I made a point of scooping up some shirts from a box and starting to walk away. "How you doing?"

"I'm glad you asked," said Amy, but I wasn't. "Well, right after school was out, I got this job dog-walking. Did you ever do that? I have to get up at seven every morning and walk three Irish setters before this woman goes to work. . . ."

"Uh-huh," I said, walking even faster.

"Then at nine thirty I . . ."

I could see Juanita frowning at me from the counter.

"I've got to take these shirts to the stockroom, Amy," I said.

"It's okay, I'll go with you," Amy said. "After I walk the Irish setters, I have to—"

"I've got work to do, Amy," I said. She's not very good at subtleties.

"I can help," said Amy.

"No. Employees only," I told her. "Bye."

When Juanita came back to the stockroom later, she said, "Your friend's still hanging around out there, Alice. Jennifer Martin gets really upset when friends come by to gab."

"She's not exactly a friend," I said, but that was unfair to Amy. "She's someone from school who's a little lost."

"Well, she'll have to get lost on her own time, not yours," Juanita said. "I'm going to tell her you've gone to lunch."

She did, and out of the small square window of the stockroom, I watched Amy turn and walk off to the children's department.

If it weren't for Les, the summer of my sophomore year would have been dullsville. I was off work on

Sunday, and Dad and Sylvia had just come home from church when Les drove up and came inside.

"He can smell lunch from sixty paces," I said as we were getting out the bagels and turkey and cheese.

"No, thanks. I had a late breakfast," Lester said, but he looked excited. Keyed up. "I just wanted to run something by you." He turned a chair away from the table and straddled it, arms resting on the back.

"Sure. What's up? Thinking of buying a new car?" Dad asked.

"More important than that," said Lester. "I'm going to ask Tracy to marry me."

Wow! I thought. But I decided that a cheer was out of place, so I just grinned and waited for Dad to say something.

"Well, well!" Dad said, a surprised smile on his face. "That *is* news! When did you decide this?"

"When I realized she's about the most wonderful woman I've ever met," Les told us.

"We like her too, Les," Sylvia said, leaning over to give him a hug. "How long have you guys known each other?"

"Eight months. I don't believe in long courtships, like some people I know," Lester teased. Dad grinned.

I didn't open my mouth for fear Les would

suddenly discover I was present and decide to continue the discussion with Dad in private. I spread mustard on my bagel in slow motion so that even the knife wouldn't attract his attention.

"Well, tell us! Have you met her family?" asked Sylvia.

Lester laughed. "Half of them, anyway. She's got relatives coming and going. Aunts, uncles, cousins, grandparents, godmother, second cousins, uncles once removed . . ."

"And do you like them?" Sylvia asked.

Les thought about that. "Yes, I do. A little reserved, maybe. Very polite. There are so many of them, I've never talked to any one person for very long."

"Well, we'll be glad to welcome Tracy into this family, Les," Dad said. "There's nothing more exciting than meeting the person you want to spend the rest of your life with."

"That's exactly how I feel," said Les.

I couldn't contain myself. "To Les and Tracy!" I said, holding up my glass of lemonade.

"I'll drink to that!" said Sylvia, and Dad smiled and lifted his glass too.

Les grinned and stood up to leave, looking pleased. Then he turned to me and gave me his stern look. "And you are *not* to say one solitary word to anyone, Al," he said. "When I'm ready to announce it, I'll let you know."

"Of course!" I said, as though the thought of rushing to the phone the moment he left and calling Liz and Pam and Gwen and Molly and Faith and Karen and Jill had never once crossed my mind.

"When do you plan to ask her, Les?" Sylvia wanted to know.

"Her birthday's later this month. I'm going to take her out to dinner, pop the question, and then we'll go shopping for a ring."

I sat grinning all through lunch. Wouldn't it be neat, I thought, if all our relatives came back for another wedding next spring? I wish *we* had relatives "coming and going." I wish *we* had aunts and uncles and grandparents and godparents and uncles once removed who could just drop in for Sunday supper or a football game on Saturday afternoons. I love Aunt Sally and Uncle Milt and Carol and Grandpa McKinley and my uncles Howard and Harold, but I wish there were more of them. In our family—Dad and Sylvia and Les and I—we sort of do things two by two. I wish there were so many of us all living in the same town that we did things six by six or eight by eight.

"You know what would be perfect?" I said finally. "A black-and-white wedding! We could have black orchids and white carnations and a chocolate wedding cake with white frosting, and all the blacks would come in white and all the whites would wear black, and—"

"And what would a mixed-race person wear? One black sock and one white one?" Dad asked. "I thought love was color-blind, Al."

And then I realized I was focusing on skin color again, and I shut up.

But Sylvia laughed. "The duty of the sister-in-law, remember, is to keep quiet and do as she's told. Whatever Lester and Tracy choose is sure to be just right for them."

At Mark's the next evening a cold front had moved in, and it wasn't a good night for swimming. We hung out for a while in the Stedmeisters' family room. Keeno cracked us up going around the room and providing captions for the old family photos perched on end tables and bookshelves.

"Madam, I believe you're standing on my foot."

"Sir, does this animal belong to you?"

"Hubert, if I've told you once, I've told you a thousand times . . ."

I'm not sure how the Stedmeisters have put up with us all these years. Pamela said she thinks they let us hang out there so much because at least they know what Mark's up to and where he is. But on this particular Monday things were falling a little flat.

Brian was driving a new car his dad had bought for him, a Toyota, and someone suggested we go over to Bethesda and check out the fountain in front of Barnes & Noble. A lot of kids hang out there on summer evenings—eat at the tables outside the Austin Grill. So we piled into three cars and headed for East-West Highway. I was sitting in the backseat of Brian's car between Liz and Gwen. Keeno was up front with Brian, and all the others were driving with Justin and Jill or Mark. When we got to B&N, though, parking was horrendous. We tried two different parking garages, but they were full, and our cell phones were going like mad as we called each other to see what to do next.

Finally we decided to head out River Road to Potomac Pizza. I'd never been on that road before. It's a wide highway, not too busy at night, with mansions set back from the street.

"Look at that one!" said Gwen, pointing to a huge white stucco house that must have had eight bedrooms, six baths, and a ballroom, floodlights illuminating the whole outside. "Do you suppose people actually live there, or is it owned by a diplomat for embassy parties?"

"And *that* one!" said Liz. "Ten bedrooms, at least!"

Up front, however, Keeno and Brian were talking horsepower.

"Sixty, man, and it's like we're crawling," Brian said. "You don't even feel the road in this baby."

Maybe Brian couldn't, but I could. I tensed up as the car went over a rise.

"Seventy-five, man, no shit!" Keeno exclaimed.

"The speed limit's forty, Brian," Gwen called.

The car kept accelerating.

"Brian, slow down!" said Liz.

"Hey, who's driving, anyway?" said Brian. "You think I want to wreck this car? Just giving it a test run, that's all." The car raced on, Keeno murmuring appreciatively.

I thought about the crosses and flowers and teddy bears I've seen on the sides of roads where teenagers have crashed—there have been a lot of wrecks here in Montgomery County. Imagined Les and Tracy's wedding taking place without me. And suddenly I said, "Brian, I'm going to throw up!"

"Hey! Not in my car!" he said, and immediately took his foot off the gas.

"Stick your head out the window!" Keeno said, laughing.

"No! I don't want puke on the side of my car!" said Brian.

"I need to get out," I told them.

The car slowed even more. I felt it pull to the right and worried that Brian was going to wreck us trying to get off in time. But finally we were rolling along the shoulder, and at last the car stopped, the emergency lights blinking.

Gwen and Liz and I got out.

"Are you really sick?" Gwen whispered.

"No, but I'm not getting back in the car with those maniacs," I said.

"Hey!" yelled Keeno. "Hurry it up."

"I'm not riding with you anymore," I declared.

"What?" said Brian. "Granny thinks I'm going too fast?"

"Just keep your eyes closed," said Keeno. "Come on."

"Not with Brian driving," I said, embarrassed and angry both.

"We can't leave you out here on the side of the road at night," said Brian.

"I've got my cell phone," I told him.

Keeno laughed. "Who you gonna call? Your daddy?"

"I think I'll call Brian's daddy to come and get us," I said angrily. "I'll tell him Brian's going eighty miles an hour in his new car in a forty-mile zone."

"Oh, get in," said Brian.

"No! You drive like an idiot!" I said.

"She's right," said Liz.

"*Every*body drives ten miles over the speed limit, at least," said Keeno.

"Not me," said Gwen.

"Look, we've lost the other cars by now. Get in and I'll go the speed limit. I promise. You can even sit up here and supervise," said Brian.

We got back in, Brian drove the speed limit, and later, when we left the pizza place, Liz and Gwen and I rode back with Jill and Justin. I realized right then how important it is to have a game plan, because you just never know.

7

What Happened on Wednesday

I got off work Tuesday at six and checked my cell phone for messages as I rode the bus home. There was just one, and it was from Chris, the guy from stage crew, Faith's new boyfriend.

Chris? I wondered, and listened: "Hi, Alice. Chris. Don't know if you're working tonight, but I thought we might get some of the gang together and take Molly to a movie. Faith talked to her this afternoon, and she said she was having a good day, so I figured it would be a good time to take her out. I'll see who else I can round up. If you're free, call me."

Chris has got to be one of the nicest guys around. Wasn't it strange, I thought, that Faith had been dating a rotten scumbag like Ron, and now she had a boyfriend like Chris? That trip to New York, where she and Chris started hanging out together, was a turning point in her life. It's weird about turning points. What they are, I mean. When they happen.

I called Chris back after I got off the bus.

"I'm in!" I said. "I'd love to go!"

"Great. Harry's coming, bringing a friend. We're going to try to make the seven thirty show—that spy flick. I forget the name. Faith says that Molly likes spy movies. Pick you up in a half hour?"

"Sure," I said.

Dad wasn't home yet and Sylvia hadn't started dinner, so I stuck a Lean Cuisine in the microwave and gulped it down with some orange juice. Sylvia was at the dining room table grading papers.

"I don't have to be at work till noon tomorrow," I told Sylvia from the doorway. "I'll call if I'm going to be later than midnight."

"Have fun," she said, and I ran upstairs to brush my teeth and put on some eyeliner.

There were six of us: Chris and Faith and Molly, Harry, his friend, and me. Harry is gay, and his friend, Max, looked so much like him that they could have been brothers. Somebody once said that we tend to choose partners who resemble ourselves. I'm not sure if that's true, but any friend of Harry's was a friend of mine, because he was the guy who came to the rescue when some knuckleheads were trying to stamp the comedy/tragedy stamp on my butt in ninth grade.

Chris drove, and Faith was squished between him and Molly in the front seat; I crawled in beside Harry and Max in back.

"Alice, Max. Max, Alice," said Harry, grinning at me as I leaned toward them to close the door after me.

"Hi, Max," I said. "Chris, this is such a good idea! I really needed a change."

"Yeah," said Faith. "Alice has to spend the whole day watching women take off their clothes."

"Doesn't sound so bad to me!" said Chris.

"Well, *I'm* psyched," said Molly. "I haven't seen a good movie in months."

"I hope you won't be disappointed," Harry said.

"Hey, it's a night out," said Molly. "And it's good to see everyone."

Unfortunately, the movie was sold out by the time we reached the window.

Chris turned toward Molly. "We can get in the nine forty-five show. You want to try for that, or is that getting too late?"

"I'm good!" said Molly.

So Chris got the tickets, and then we ambled around the mall.

"You sure you're up for this?" Faith asked Molly as we paused at a music store and Chris looked at CDs in the window.

"Yeah, so far I'm holding up," Molly said. She

ran one hand through her hair, then automatically checked her fingers. "It's nuts, I know, but I worry most about losing my hair. And the doctor says I will. Comes with the territory. I might not lose it all, he says, but . . . I don't know. No hair might look better than clumps of it here and there."

Harry held up one finger. "Idea!" he said, and took Molly by the arm. We followed along, and he led us to a new store called Lids that sold nothing but caps. Not hats. Caps. Every kind of cap you could think of. We started to smile as we went inside.

"Okay," said Harry, hands on Molly's shoulders, studying her face. "Max, what do you think?"

"Hmmm," said his friend. "I'd go for the blue with the silver trim."

"Really?" said Harry. "How about the blue with beads on the bill?"

Chris took a black baseball cap with buttons all over it, one from every state, and set it on Molly's head.

"No," said Faith, snatching it off and putting a red satin cap on her instead. "Something sexy she can wear with satin underwear."

"Yeah, right," said Molly, laughing. She modeled each cap as though she were on a fashion runway, and we ended up buying two—a blue denim with signs of the zodiac embroidered all over it and a black number with red sequins.

"Hey, thanks, you guys!" Molly said. "They're terrific!"

We goofed around till the next show, and then we sat at the back, whispering comments to each other about the thriller on the screen. Once you're involved in stage stuff, I guess, you're always the critic, and when Harry and Max started guessing who the mole was, Molly joked that she would get the manager if they didn't let her figure it out herself.

It had a surprise ending, though, that tricked us all, and the surprise of *our* evening was that when we got Molly back to her house, she looked even more energetic than she had at the start as she grinned at us from the porch, waving a cap in each hand.

Pam and Liz and Gwen and Yolanda had an early dinner with me the next day on my break. Pamela didn't get as long a break as I did, so the others already had a table saved for us when we met them in the food court outside Burger King.

Liz had been reading a magazine article that supposedly analyzed your personality based on your favorite color.

"Okay, Gwen, what's yours?" Liz asked.

"Oh, yellow, I suppose," said Gwen.

Liz ran her finger down the page till she found it.

"Yellow," she repeated. "You are idealistic, cheerful, and a good planner. What's yours, Pamela?"

"Purple?" said Pam.

"Temperamental, unique, and sensitive," Liz read.

"What's *your* favorite color, Liz?" I asked.

"Blue."

"And . . . ?"

She found it and made a face: "Capable, conservative, and inclined to caution."

"Each of these colors has exactly three attributes?" asked Gwen.

"I guess so. I didn't write the article," said Liz. "Yolanda?"

"I'll go with black," Yolanda said.

"Hmmm," said Liz. "Dignity, wit, and cleverness."

"*Yolanda?*" shrieked Gwen, and Yolanda gave her hand a slap.

"What about you, Alice?" asked Gwen.

"Green, of course."

"You are frank, stable, and persistent," said Liz.

"Ugh, ugh, and ugh," I said. "Now, *that's* exciting."

"This stuff could apply to anyone," said Gwen. "I'll bet at least one of those qualities from every color could apply to all of us."

"I had a dream once where everything was purple," Yolanda said.

"You dream in Technicolor?" asked Pamela. "I think all my dreams are in black and white."

I'd never thought much about color in my dreams and tried to remember. "Last night," I told them, "I dreamed that Sylvia had a baby. And she's had a hysterectomy. How's that for drama?"

"Maybe you want a little sister," said Liz. "I never wanted a sibling till Nathan was born, and now I wouldn't mind having another one."

Yolanda was frowning, though. "It may not be as happy a dream as you think, Alice," she said. "You know what they say: If you dream about death, it means there will be a birth. But if you dream about a birth, it means that someone you know is going to die."

Gwen doesn't have much patience with superstitions. "Oh, come on, girl! Of course someone she knows will die! Everybody's going to die, so what else is new?"

Yolanda shrugged. Gwen was right, of course. But something like that stays with you whether you want it to or not. All I could think of was Molly.

Pamela changed the subject.

"Dad said maybe he'd take me to the ocean before school starts," she said. "He's suddenly being very nice to me these days. I think it has something to do with Meredith."

"The nurse?" I asked. "The girlfriend?"

"Yeah." Pamela picked up a piece of cheese and popped it into her mouth. "She was in the bathroom when I got up this morning, by the way."

We looked at Pamela.

"That means . . . ?" said Liz.

"Yeah. That she was there all night. With Dad, I mean. I got up to pee about five, and she was just coming out, dressed in her hospital scrubs. I think she was embarrassed I saw her."

"What does she expect? It's your bathroom!" I said.

"What did you *say*?" asked Elizabeth.

"Nothing. I was hardly awake. I just went inside and shut the door," said Pamela.

"What did *she* say?" asked Gwen.

"I'm not sure. 'Excuse me,' maybe. It was so weird. Now I wonder how many other times she's stayed overnight and left early and I didn't even know she was there. I think she works the three to eleven shift." She picked up a piece of onion and stuffed that in her mouth too. "I don't know why I had to be born into that family."

"So did your dad say anything to you?" asked Yolanda.

"Not a word. Maybe he doesn't know I saw her. I'm positive he doesn't want *Mom* to know. She'd spaz."

"But the divorce went through!" I said. "It's final!"

"I don't think you ever get divorced emotionally, though," Pamela said. "So now I've got this big secret I have to keep from her. It's crazy."

"Not as crazy as *my* dad," said Yolanda. "His girl-friend's been living with us for three years, and I'm supposed to call her 'Mom' and tell everyone they're married. Yeah, right."

What exactly makes a family? I wondered. A bunch of people living under the same roof? A bunch of related individuals under separate roofs? Same race? Same nationality? Or can a family be as mixed up and unique as the people in it?

After I'd said good-bye to my friends and was heading back inside Hecht's, I saw Tracy coming out.

"Tracy!" I said.

"Well! Alice!" she said. "I kept my eye out for you but didn't know where you'd be working."

"I'm in misses' sportswear now," I said. "You shopping?"

"Trying to. I've got a special occasion coming up and need a dress. Can't decide on a color."

My mind took her words in like a computer, sifting and sorting and lining them up. Her birth-day. Did she sense this was going to be special, I wondered? That Lester was going to propose? Les liked her in bright colors, I knew that much.

"I'd go with red or yellow," I said. "You look good in both."

She laughed. "You ever try to find a red dress in the summertime? But I'll keep looking. Hecht's didn't have anything I really want."

"Good luck!" I told her, and smiled to myself. It's hard to pretend you don't know anything when the whole scenario is playing out in your head: Lester in a sport coat, Tracy in a red or yellow dress, the dinner, the proposal, the ring . . .

At the moment our department was between sales, so we were virtually empty over the dinner hour. Things didn't pick up later, either, and I had to look for things to keep me busy. Juanita had just gone on break when I saw three customers over in designer jeans. One was a fiftyish man and the others were younger women, one white, one black. I thought of the time Liz and Gwen and I were shopping together and the store detective had singled out Gwen and followed her around.

I smiled at the black woman, and she smiled back as they browsed. *You're lucky I'm working tonight,* I was thinking. *You're going to get the same respect I'd give anyone.*

I straightened a rack of shirts and helped another customer find a top. I glanced again at the customers over in designer jeans and saw only the man this time, studying a label. I picked up an armful of empty hangers that had collected behind the counter and took them back to the box in the fitting rooms. The two women I'd seen earlier weren't there, either.

As I came out onto the floor again, I swerved and made a detour around knit tops to collect a stray hanger at the end of a rack. I passed one of the aisles and caught a glimpse of the two women stooping low over a shopping bag, and as I walked on toward the counter, I suddenly realized what I had seen.

The more I thought about it, the more sure I was. The fiftyish man was their lookout. One woman had been holding open a huge shopping bag, and the other was shoving armfuls of designer jeans inside it. *Booster bag.*

My tongue seemed stuck to my teeth and my pulse raced. I glanced around for Juanita but knew she was still on her break. A trickle of sweat ran down my back.

I picked up the phone and punched in the security code, trying to remember the code word for "theft in progress."

"Security," came a voice at the other end, but before I could make a sound, a large hand clamped down over mine and lowered the phone to its cradle. The steel gray eyes of the middle-aged man bore into mine.

All I could think of right then was Yolanda's warning that someone I knew was going to die. *Me*, who else? He didn't let go, just stood there pressing my hand down hard on the telephone, while the women's heads bobbed up again. With lightning speed, they emptied another shelf into a second shopping bag, and then they separated, one going toward the south exit, the other toward the east.

I desperately scanned the area—infants and toddlers across the way, women's shoes farther down—but saw only one other clerk with her back toward me.

Suddenly the man let go of my hand and, without a word, walked quickly, but still casually, out of my department and disappeared. Seconds later the store detective came sprinting up, and I was still hyperventilating.

"A man . . . about fifty. . . . He was with two women. One went that way and one the other. They've got two shopping bags full of designer jeans," I panted. "I think the man went toward the escalator . . . I'm not sure."

The detective used his walkie-talkie and directed security personnel to cover the parking lots. I gave him the best descriptions I could before he took off again, but my knees were still shaking when Juanita came back.

"What's going on?" she asked.

"Shoplifters," I told her. "Right after you left."

"Wouldn't you know!" she said. "Chances are they checked out this department in advance. They knew who was on duty and when we took our breaks."

"But I wasn't even able to say what was happening when I called security," I said. "The man pushed the phone back down and held it there. How did the detective know where to come?"

"Security can tell which extension you're on, and they send the store detective to your area if you don't respond," she said. "Did he actually touch the phone? They might want to dust it for prints."

"I'm not sure," I said.

"Hey!" said Juanita. "Looks like they've got someone."

I turned toward the escalators, and sure enough, the detective was escorting the man, his hands locked behind him.

"This the man?" the detective asked.

The steel gray eyes fixed themselves on me, and I felt he would have strangled me on the spot if I spoke. I nodded.

"If this is who we think he is, we've been looking

for this trio for a *looooong* time," the detective said.

The store manager came hurrying over. "They get the other two?"

The detective was listening on his walkie-talkie. "The county police are out there now, and they've got the exits blocked," he said.

Juanita looked at me. "Alice, let's sit down," she said. "You look like you don't have a drop of blood in your body."

I didn't even want her to use my name. I didn't want the man with the gray eyes to know anything about me. We walked over to the two chairs next to the fitting rooms, and I sat down.

"What do they *do* with all the stuff they walked out with?" I asked her.

"Sell it to mom-and-pop stores in New York. There're a dozen different ways to cash in on it."

They caught the white woman a half hour later trying to leave the parking lot on foot, then the black woman hiding in the man's van. It was packed with loot they'd stolen from other shopping malls, the police said.

It took me some time to breathe normally and process what had happened. What if I hadn't come out of the fitting rooms when I had and seen what was going on? What if I hadn't made that detour to get that hanger? And then, more important, why hadn't I *guessed*? In the training session they'd warned us about thieves traveling in groups. What was the man doing in women's designer jeans in the first place? Why hadn't I gone over to check?

"Thieves come in all shapes and sizes and colors," Sergeant Camfield had told us. But I had been so eager to be fair that I forgot.

8

Utter Humiliation

At last I had something exciting to tell the family at dinner. Dad and Sylvia had held off eating until I got home, and the incident disturbed them more than I'd thought.

"I don't like the idea of your being left in a department by yourself at night," Dad said. "They should have a person trained in emergency procedures on duty all the time."

"It's not possible, Dad!" I told him. "Even the most experienced salespeople have to take breaks sometime."

"Do you think you'll be called as a witness?" Sylvia wanted to know.

I shook my head. "They found the two women with the jeans in their bags. That should be evidence enough."

"What about the man?" asked Dad.

"The police said that the three of them have

been working as a team, and they've left a trail from Ohio to Maryland. Stores have their pictures on security cameras."

"Well, I'm glad they're caught," said Dad. "That kind of excitement I can do without."

Les hadn't come by, though, so I called him later. "You missed one of the most exciting episodes of my life," I said. "Why weren't you here for dinner?"

"Al, I've been eating there more than I have in my own apartment," he said. "Sylvia's going to start charging if I don't quit mooching off them. Why? What happened at dinner? You swallow your braces or something?"

"I was responsible for catching a gang of thieves at Hecht's, Lester!" I said.

"You're joking."

"No! Shoplifters!" At last I had his attention. "And when the ringleader realized I was calling store security, he grabbed me and ordered me to stop."

"*What?*"

"Well, actually, he grabbed my arm . . . my *hand,* anyway . . . well, the *telephone,* and he made me hang up."

"And *then*?" Lester prodded.

"Security could tell where the call had come from and sent the store detective to check. And they caught all three of them—one man and two women!"

"And you did all that without passing out or throwing up? Way to go, Al!" Lester said.

Of course I had to e-mail everyone I knew. The next afternoon I even phoned Rosalind, my old friend from grade school over in Takoma Park. I found that we both had a day off. I told her about all the excitement.

"They give you a raise?" she asked.

"Hardly."

"Well, let's celebrate!" said Rosalind. She's always in the mood to celebrate something. "What do you want to do? See a movie? Throw a Frisbee? Take a walk?"

"A walk sounds good," I said. "I haven't done much running this week. Let's go to the park."

"Okay. I've got an errand to run for Mom, and then I'll drive over," she told me.

"Take your time," I said. It's always good to see Rosalind. We go to different schools, have different friends, but we still see each other now and then.

I sat down at my computer and tried to think if there was anyone else I wanted to tell about the shoplifting incident. I'd wait to tell Molly when I saw her again. Give us something new to talk about. Then I decided to check my in-box while I waited for Rosalind.

One e-mail telling me I'd won seventy thousand dollars in a lottery. Yeah, right. Delete. One selling medicines online and another address I didn't recognize. The subject line read: *Your future love life predicted here.*

I grinned. I love those quizzes that are supposed to tell you all kinds of stuff about yourself. About as reliable as tea leaves in a cup, but who *wouldn't* want to know her future, especially in the sex department? I clicked on *Start* and read the first paragraph on the page I linked to:

> Answer the following questions to predict what your future love life will be like. You may be surprised and delighted to discover the sensual side of yourself. Your analysis will appear at the end and will depend entirely on your honesty, so answer truthfully.

I scrolled down to the first question:

1. How many times have you had sex?

Define sex, I thought. They sure got to the point in a hurry. Was fooling around under a boy's jacket at night on a bus from New York considered sex? I studied the choices given:

a. Never
b. Once
c. Two or three times
d. More than five

I clicked on *Never.*

2. Have you ever undressed for a
guy?
a. No
b. Partially
c. All the way

No, I clicked.

3. Have you ever given a guy head?
a. No
b. Once
c. More than once
d. More than one guy

It occurred to me that all these questions were
directed to girls. There was probably a separate set
for guys, I decided. I wondered how the computer
knew. I clicked *No.*

4. Have you ever been intimately
touched by a guy?

a. No
b. Yes
c. More than once
d. More than one guy

I chose *c.* Sam.

5. How many times a week do you mas-
turbate?

My God, this was so personal! *Lie,* I thought.
But I looked at the top of that screen where it said
I had to be honest to get the right analysis, so I
studied the choices:

a. None
b. One
c. Two or three
d. Every day

Blushing, I clicked on *Two or three.*

6. Which sexual activity would you be
willing to try?
a. Group sex
b. Anal sex
c. Oral sex
d. Intercourse with a dog

A *dog*? The only one I was curious about was *c.*

> 7. Do you ever dream about having sex
> with guys you know?
> a. Yes
> b. No
> c. Sometimes

Sometimes, I responded.

Your answers are being analyzed, the screen read.
Click SUBMIT, then NEXT. I obeyed.

Instantly, the screen lit up like a neon sign with
lightbulbs blinking around a theater marquee. In
big orange letters I read:

> THE JOKE'S ON YOU! YOUR ANSWERS
> HAVE BEEN FORWARDED TO BRIAN
> BREWSTER.

I gave a little scream, and my face grew as hot as
the letters. *Here's what you wrote,* it read on the
screen, and there were my answers, along with my
name, for all the world to see.

I scooted away from the computer, gasping for
breath, and heard Sylvia answer the door downstairs.

"Alice?" she called. "Rosalind's on her way up."

I covered my mouth and stared wildly at the

screen as Rosalind's footsteps sounded on the stairs. Then my round, funny friend was standing in my doorway in her tank top and shorts, giving me her puzzled grin.

It disappeared as soon as she saw my face. "What's the matter?" she asked.

I pressed my hands to my burning cheeks. "Brian!" I cried. "I *hate* him!"

"Who? What is it?" she asked, walking over.

I threw myself over the screen so she wouldn't see it, my face hotter still.

"What the heck . . . ?" said Rosalind.

And then . . . I started to cry. Brian and Mark and Keeno and Justin and—oh God! maybe even Patrick—and who knows who else were going to know the most personal, intimate things about me! What did it matter if Rosalind saw them? I crumpled into a fetal position, head in my lap. I could sense that Roz was reading the screen.

"Oh, man," she said. "I've heard about this one."

I reared up. *"What?"*

"This trick, this Web site, 'The Joke's on You!' You can send any kind of thing to somebody and make them think it came from some anonymous place that doesn't even know you. But your reply goes back to your so-called friend."

*"Every*one will see it!" I wept. "He'll send it out

to *every*one!" I was practically spitting out the words. I felt like my hair was on fire, I was so furious. "I could *kill* him, Rosalind!"

"No need for that," said Roz. "Exit and get back on this Web site again."

"*Why?*"

"Just do it! Trust me!"

I rolled my chair up to the computer, closed the page, then went to my "Old Mail" folder and accessed the e-mail titled *Your future love life predicted here.* Clicking on *Start* took me to the quiz again.

"Now what?" I cried. "There's no way I can delete what I already sent."

"Scroll back down to the questions."

"*What?*"

"You're going to send him second and third and fourth replies, like you're having the time of your life."

"Are you nuts?"

"No. Go ahead. We have to make it look like you sent one right after the other. Answer the first one: 'How many times have you had sex?' Click on 'More than five.'"

"Rosalind . . . !"

"Just do it," she said, so I did.

"'Have you ever undressed for a guy?' Click . . . Oh, let's click 'Partially.' We're going to get Brian, whoever he is, so mixed up, he won't know if he's coming or going."

I began to get the drift. "He'll always know that the first one was the real one," I sniffled, my cheeks still wet.

"Not necessarily," said Rosalind.

By the time we got down to how many times a week I masturbated, Rosalind made me select *Every day.*

I clicked on the SUBMIT button and started all over again. We sent him one in which I denied doing anything—I'd never been touched, never had sexy dreams—and one in which I went overboard on every question. By the time we'd sent off number five, I felt drained and logged off the computer.

"I still hate him," I said.

"I know."

"What if he comes up to me in front of everyone and says, 'So you're ready to try oral sex, huh?' What will I *say?*"

"Say, 'No, Brian! I said I wanted to do it with a dog, don't you remember?'"

I smiled a little. "I should take you around with me for the next month or so. I never think up the right answer till it's too late. He's such a creep. And I'm an idiot for falling for it."

"Don't ever spill your secrets online," Rosalind

told me. "They're always going to get out. Now, you ready for that walk in the park?"

I put on my sneakers and we went outside. I couldn't believe it. At that exact same moment, guess who was riding by on his way to his job at the pizza place? Just like in the movies, there was Brian's car, his arm resting on the open window.

"That's *him—Brian*!" I gasped, poking Rosalind.

She must have taken over my psyche, because suddenly I heard myself yelling, "Hey, Brian! I just sent you some e-mail!"

The car slowed, and he gave me a cautious smile. "Yeah?"

"Yeah, that trick's a month old, at least," Roz called out.

"Just wanted to liven up your day!" I said pleasantly as we climbed in Rosalind's car.

And you know what? *Brian's* face got red, and he speeded up and turned the corner. We burst out laughing. "Next best thing to catching *him* with his pants down," said Rosalind.

What I liked most about my friend right then was that she never asked me a thing about my answers to those questions. Never commented. It was like she knew she had come upon private stuff that was meant to be kept private and that my secrets were safe with her. Always before, it seemed, when Rosalind came over to play back in grade school, I ended up getting in trouble. This time she saved my butt.

"You're the best," I told her.

She grinned. "I know it," she said.

I was too embarrassed about my stupidity to tell Sylvia about it. I did warn Pamela, Liz, and Gwen, luckily, because Liz had found the same thing on her computer.

But after Dad and Sylvia went out that evening, I was still hating life—Brian, in particular—when Aunt Sally called from Chicago.

"So what's going on out there in Silver Spring, sweetheart?" she asked, and I told her about the shoplifting incident at work. I could hear her rapid "Oh my! Oh my!" And then, "Just think! You'll get your picture in the paper and everything. No, *don't* let them put your picture in the paper, Alice, or your name, either. You don't want those shoplifters looking you up when they get out of prison."

I laughed a little. "Don't worry, Aunt Sally. The store's taking all the credit for catching those guys. I don't get so much as a doughnut for my coffee break."

Having said that, why did I want to confide in Aunt Sally about the e-mail Brian had sent me? I guess I just wanted to vent until every bit of hate had spilled out, because it was like poison, eating away at my gut.

"Listen," I said. "You know what was even worse than that? Some guy I know found out some very personal stuff about me, and I know he's going to tell all his friends."

"Well, that's awful!" said Aunt Sally. "Did he go through your purse or what?"

"No . . . it's something I said in an e-mail," I told her.

"An e-mail? Over the Internet?" Aunt Sally cried. "Oh, Alice, the Internet's worse than shoplifters! Why, a girl in Indiana was driven off in a panel truck by a man she wrote to on e-mail, and she was never seen again. A widow in South Carolina sold her house to marry a man who proposed to her on the Internet, and it turned out he was married with eleven children."

"Don't worry, I learned my lesson," I said. "But I'll never get over the humiliation."

"Well, let me tell you what happened to me back in eighth grade," said Aunt Sally. "I was having my period and kept an extra pad in my pocketbook. That's a purse, you know. In my day we didn't have backpacks. In homeroom, if the teacher hadn't come in yet, the boys had a habit of standing just inside the door and teasing us girls as we came in. One morning they'd try to grab our caps or gloves;

another day, they'd try to kiss some of us. They'd trip us or something."

"Sounds more like fourth grade," I told her.

"Well, we weren't exactly mature back then," she said. "On this particular day, though, they were try- ing to grab our pocketbooks. And as I came in, they grabbed mine. First they threw it around the room like a football, from one boy to another, as I tried to get it back. Then some guy took it over in the corner and started taking stuff out."

I knew what was coming.

"He found my lipstick," Aunt Sally went on, "and put some on his face. Then he found my pad, and when he realized what it was, he yelled, 'Hey, Tom! Catch!' And he threw it to the next guy. As soon as it hit Tom's chest, he was embarrassed too and threw it to someone else, trying to get rid of it fast. My sanitary pad was getting battered from boy to boy, and it wasn't long before every- one knew what it was and that it was mine."

"Omigod!" I said.

"I wanted to die, Alice," said Aunt Sally. "If the floor had opened just then and swallowed me, I would have been glad. But then the pad started to come apart just as the teacher walked in. He was late and feeling crabby and yelled, 'What *is* this stuff?' Somebody said, 'It's Sally's,' so he said to me, 'Pick it up.'"

Listening to Aunt Sally, I could feel my face burning—for her. "What did you say?" I asked.

"I just sat there, my face getting redder and redder. I couldn't get out a single word. The teacher was busy, sorting stuff on his desk, and I had to go around the room picking up the remains of that pad while the boys smirked and the girls sat like statues, dying with me."

We were both quiet for a moment, each reliving our most embarrassing moments. I was thinking how there is about a forty-year age difference between Aunt Sally and me, yet her humiliation back then was just as intense as mine now.

"It's hard for me to realize I used to be so shy," she said at last. "Today I wouldn't have stood for that for a moment. I would have gone to that teacher and told him it was something personal that the boys had stolen from my purse. But . . . I didn't." Then she added, "Boys can be really stupid sometimes. I think it has something to do with their trousers."

"What?" I said.

"I think that boys and men go around their whole lives being uncomfortable," she said. "Just think about it, Alice—all they've got between their legs."

Had she really said that? I wondered, but she barreled right on. "If anyone should wear a skirt for comfort, it's a man. But instead, he's got this seam in his trousers down there, always pulling at him, and I think this has something to do with his brain, I really do. Now, *some* cultures got it right. Look at the Africans and their loincloths! Look at the Egyptians and their robes! Look at the Scots and their kilts! Why, when your uncle gets irritable and grumpy, Alice, I say, 'Milt, go take a nice hot soak in the tub and put on your bathrobe.' And you know, that just calms him right down. I say it's the trousers binding them down there that makes them do these ridiculous things. That and neckties. Get rid of trousers and neckties, I always say, and we'll have a more peaceful world."

I couldn't help smiling. "I can't wait to point that out to Dad and Lester, Aunt Sally," I said. "I'm so glad you called."

9

Talk

Pamela called and said her dad really was taking her to the ocean the third weekend in August—it would be a four-day weekend, actually, and he'd said she could invite two friends. She was inviting Liz and me. That was at least *one* nice thing I had to look forward to over the summer.

"Great! Sounds good!" I said. "Remember when *my* dad took us to the ocean?" I was thinking of the summer between sixth and seventh grades, when Patrick had become my boyfriend. "You and Liz and me? It'll be like old times."

I could hear her chuckle over the phone. "And Lester surprised us by showing up later with Patrick?"

"And *you* tried to crawl in bed with Patrick to make him think it was me and got Lester instead?" I reminded her, and we both laughed at the memory.

"I'd sure like to crawl in bed with Les now," Pamela said. "I wouldn't be in such a hurry to crawl out again, let me tell you."

I *almost* told her that Lester was getting himself engaged, but I stopped myself in time.

"You working tomorrow?" Pamela asked me.

"Yeah, ten to six, and then I'm going to drive over to see Molly. Sylvia's letting me have her car for the day," I said.

"I'm on the noon to nine shift, so I can't go with you," Pamela told me. "I'll concentrate on Rehoboth Beach. We'll have a blast."

The next morning I dressed for work and went downstairs for the car keys.

"Thanks, Sylvia," I said. "I don't know how long I'll be at Molly's. They invited me for dinner, too, so it might be a while."

"Stay as long as you like," she said. She was standing on a step stool in shorts and a T-shirt, cleaning out cupboard shelves up near the ceiling. "You know, these are so high, they're almost useless. I'm thinking of taking out this whole back wall when we remodel and adding a family room. What do you think?"

"I think that whatever you and Dad decide, you're going to do anyway, so what I say won't have much effect," I said breezily.

I could tell by the look on her face that this hadn't come out quite right.

"Alice, your opinion definitely counts," she said. "We want you to be in on the planning too."

"Sure!" I said. "Let me see the floor plan the way you want it, and I'll put in my two cents. I like the idea of a family room as part of the kitchen."

"Do you?" She was pleased. "I'll work up something and show it to you." As I picked up the car keys, she said, "I think Ben and I will go out for dinner since you're eating at Molly's. If Les comes by, he's out of luck."

"It won't hurt him to cook for himself a little more," I said, and went on out to the car.

It irked me sometimes that Sylvia just seemed to be barreling ahead with plans for renovating the house, and whatever she wanted was fine with Dad. I couldn't believe he'd give in as easily as he had. If she decided one day that she wanted a study with a stone fireplace up to the ceiling, that was fine with him. What if she decided to put in a bowling alley? Was he just going to lie down and roll over?

But, of course, I didn't say anything either. Whatever Sylvia wanted was seemingly fine with me too. We were still so polite with each other. Sometimes I thought that what Sylvia and I needed was a real out-and-out argument. Yelling and everything. And when it was over, if we were still friends, maybe then I'd truly believe we were family. When you live with your birth mother, she sort of has to love you, no matter what. But if it's your stepmom, how do you ever know for sure?

Juanita was wearing a new summer outfit when I got to work, a coral linen skirt and top that accentuated her dark hair.

"You're gorgeous," I told her, and her face crinkled in pleasure.

"I got a few clothes on sale," she said. "We're going to Puerto Rico in September—two whole weeks. Are you going to get away at all?"

"I'm going to the ocean with a friend!" I said. "It would be more fun if her dad wasn't along, but I guess you can't have everything."

We were busy all day, and Juanita said it would be like this for the rest of the month; we had all the summer stock to get rid of, all the final markdowns, while new fall stuff was coming in every day. If I wasn't moving racks of clothes around, I was marking down price tags, rearranging new shipments, constantly removing garments from fitting rooms and getting them back on the sale racks. I'd had only a thirty-minute break for lunch and was in no mood to see Amy Sheldon coming toward me halfway through the afternoon.

I was all ready to tell her she couldn't come by anymore when I saw tears streaming down her face. Her bottom lip trembled.

"Amy?" I said.

"Brian did something awful," she said, a little too loudly, and several customers turned and stared.

I looked around for Juanita. "Could I take my break?" I asked. "This is sort of an emergency."

She saw Amy trailing behind me. "Fifteen minutes, Alice, tops."

"I'll be back," I said, and led Amy over to the women's room. I'd already guessed what she had to tell me. We sat down on a little couch at one side. "What happened?" I asked.

"He sent me this thing on my e-mail, and I didn't know it was him!" she wept.

I nodded sympathetically. "Oh, that," I said. "He tricked me, too."

She stared. "He *did*? Did you tell him all that body stuff? It said it would predict my love life! I just wanted to know."

"So did I. He's a jerk, Amy."

"But he's telling everyone. I'm getting e-mails from boys I don't even know. They want me to do dirty things with them. My dad asked me about the notes—about what I've been doing." Her eyes were streaming tears again and her nose was running.

Of all the girls at school, Amy Sheldon was probably the least able to defend herself. I just reached out and hugged her. She sobbed. If I could have grabbed Brian by the balls right then and squeezed, I would have.

"We're going to get even some way, Amy," I told her.

"I'd slap him, but he'd slap me back," she said.

"You don't have to slap him. I'll think of something," I said. I got her a tissue and sat with her until she stopped crying. Then I walked her to an exit and hugged her again.

When six o'clock finally came, I was ready for the day to be over, in more ways than one. Just when I thought I wouldn't have to waste one more minute obsessing over Brian's stupid sex quiz, it was beating big-time in my head. I went out to the car and sank down in the driver's seat, exhaling in one long, continuous breath.

Then I turned the key in the ignition and nothing happened. Absolutely nothing. The engine was totally, utterly, completely dead.

I threw back my head and howled: "Arrrggghhh." That didn't help.

I took the key out, inserted it again, and turned. Nothing. It was as though someone had broken in while I was at work and stolen the engine. What did I do now?

I looked hopefully around. People were hurrying in and out of the mall, either trying to get home in time for dinner or squeezing a little shopping in over the dinner hour. No one even glanced my way.

Taking my cell phone from my bag, I quickly dialed home, hoping I could catch Dad or Sylvia before they went out, but it was too late. Only the answering machine. "Hello, this is Sylvia McKinley. Neither Ben nor Alice nor I can come to the phone right now. Please leave a message and we'll call you back." *Beep.*

I punched END on the cell phone, my pulse beginning to race. I thought about going back in the store to find someone who could help, but our department was a madhouse. The whole store was, in fact, with our big two-day sale. Did we have AAA? Dad did, I think. Did that include Sylvia or me? I didn't know.

So I did the only thing left to do. I called Lester.

George Palamas, one of his housemates, answered. "Alice?" he said. "Les is grilling some steaks outside. Hold on and I'll take the phone out there."

There were the sounds of footsteps, the slam of a door, outside noises, and then Lester's voice: "This better be important," he said. "I've got one medium, one rare, and one medium rare, and we paid plenty for these, so I've got a short attention span at the moment. What do you want?"

"I just got off work, and Sylvia's car won't start," I said.

I could hear him exhale. I could almost feel his breath. "Al, do you have a sixth sense or what? How do you manage to call at the most inopportune times? I need three hands here."

"I'm sorry, but I didn't know what else to do!" I said meekly.

"Do any lights come on? Anything on the dashboard to tell you what's wrong?"

"Nothing! It doesn't even make a sound. I think maybe someone stole the engine while I was at work," I said.

"What?" he said.

"I don't hear anything at all, Lester. Not a clunk or a clink."

"Just a minute, Al. I've got to turn one of these steaks."

"What should I *do?*" I wailed softly.

"So look under the hood and see if there's an engine!" he said in exasperation. "Give me a minute here before I burn something. . . ."

I laid my cell phone on the seat, sprang the hood latch, and got out. I went around to the front of the car and opened the hood. Everything was still there, I guessed. At least, I didn't see any empty spaces or disconnected cables.

I slid back in the car and picked up my cell

phone. "The engine's still there," I told him.

He gasped. "You mean you *checked*?"

"You *said*!"

"God almighty."

"So what should I do?"

"Put the key in the ignition again."

I did. "Okay," I told him.

"Turn it."

I turned. "Nothing," I said. "I *told* you!"

"Is the gearshift in park?"

I looked. "It's on 'D,'" I said. Then I knew. *D* was for *drive*. I moved the gearshift to *P*. I turned the key again. The engine caught.

"I hear an engine," said Les. "Al, wasn't that one of the first things we taught you? Whenever the car won't start, your first thought should be to check if it's in park, not to check for a stolen engine."

"I'm sorry, Lester!" I mewed, embarrassed. "Go back to your steaks. Go back to your friends. Go back to your life and—"

"Stuff it, Al," he said. "Just remember: 'P' is for 'park.'"

Molly looked as though she'd been crying when I came in. I could tell by her quick, artificial smile that I'd caught her off guard. Maybe she hadn't heard her mom answer the door. She was lying across her bed when I got upstairs.

"Maybe you haven't had such a good day," I said cautiously, sitting down in a chair by her window.

Her voice wavered a little. "No day is a good day anymore," she said. "But I'm not going to lay that on you."

"Why not? I'd rather hear how you really feel than what you think I want to hear," I told her.

I was surprised then to see tears gathering in her eyes, the way her mouth sagged at the corners, her chin trembling as she tried not to cry. "It's just so . . . so . . . how I don't want it to be," she wept, grabbing a tissue and sitting up to blow her nose. "I'm sorry, Alice. I had chemo this morning, and I always feel sick afterward."

"Don't be sorry, be mad! I feel good that you can tell me."

"What can I say?" Molly said brokenly. "I can't say, 'Why me?' because other people get cancer too. But I . . . just feel . . . as though my body's turned against me. And when you can't even trust your*self* . . ."

I nodded.

"I had big plans for this summer! I was going to work at the stables on Beach Drive. They have a program for teaching handicapped kids to ride, and I so wanted to do that. And I'd signed up to be a tutor for anyone needing help in science over the summer. Now look at me! I get tired out just going up and down stairs."

"Will you get some energy back as the treatment goes along?" I asked.

"No, less. Especially when I'm nauseated. That's almost worse than anything. Well, that and my hair."

"I'd hate that too," I said. Her hair didn't look bad to me, but I did notice some on her pillow.

She wiped her eyes. "I'm jumping ahead, I know. Maybe if I don't feel any worse than I do now, it won't be too bad." She managed a little smile, so I smiled back.

"You're a fighter, Molly! You're going to give those cancer cells everything you've got." I was remembering the way she had charged at Faith's boyfriend last April when he pounded Faith's face against the hood of his car. "If you go at them like you went at Ron, they don't have a chance."

We both laughed then.

"I'm glad you came over, Alice," she said, her blue eyes clear again. "It's like my life has been divided between *before* I got leukemia and *after*. Everyone says that, I know. And yet . . . when I go to the clinic, I see kids who seem a whole lot sicker than me. And then I wonder if that will be me someday. Bald and pale and string-bean skinny."

"What does the doctor say?" I asked.

"He's optimistic. He says there's a lot in my favor—something about hyperdiploidy and other stuff I can't pronounce. He's all smiles when he sees me, and I tell myself he wouldn't be so cheerful if I was going to die."

"No, I doubt it," I said, though I wasn't at all sure.

"Girls," called her mom. "We're going to eat out on the porch tonight. There's a breeze, and I thought you might enjoy that."

"Sure," said Molly, getting up, and we went downstairs.

Mr. Brennan was a large man who had an Irish look about him—the opposite of his wife, who was small and dark. He beamed at me as he passed the turkey salad and sliced tomatoes. "Never eat hot food on a screened porch," he said. "Cancels out the breeze." I smiled. "You got a big family, Alice?"

"Just Dad and Lester and me, and our step-mother."

"You mean your dad got by with only one daughter?" Mr. Brennan cast his eyes upward in mock despair. "Lord, what did I do to deserve five?"

I looked questioningly at Molly, and her mother said, "Molly has four older sisters. Two are here in the area, and Avis and Joan are out on the West Coast—California and Oregon."

"Avis is coming to see me next week," said Molly. "And Joan's coming for the whole month of September."

"That's great," I said. "I always wanted a sister." And I smiled to myself as I thought of Tracy.

I told them about the shoplifting incident at work and about how I hadn't been able to start the car before I came over that day, but I didn't tell them about Amy. I'd stick to good news, and it was good to see Molly laugh. She'd eaten only a few bites of her dinner, though, and then, near the end, a few bites more. Her mom had made a pineapple custard for dessert, and Molly managed to eat most of that. But after we went back to her room, she excused herself and threw up in the toilet.

When she came back to her room, she said, "You don't ever have to worry about me being bulimic, Alice," she said. "Next to being dizzy, throwing up is my least favorite thing to do."

I invited Gwen, Liz, and Pamela over for the night on Sunday. Liz had a henna painting kit, and she and Pamela were making intricate designs on their hands.

"She just looked miserable," I said, after telling them about my evening at Molly's. "I'm so used to seeing her energetic and enthusiastic about everything. Now she just drags up the stairs."

"So why did God pick on Molly?" asked Pamela. "She probably doesn't have an enemy in the whole school, unless it's Ron. Good grades, great personality . . ."

"It's not like God *wants* her to suffer. It just might be that some greater good will come out of her having leukemia," offered Liz.

"Wait a minute," I said. "Molly has to get sick to help God—who is all-powerful—to accomplish something?"

We thought about that a minute.

"I think leukemia just happens," said Gwen. "It's like an earthquake, a tsunami, a tornado. Nature doesn't think about humans who get in the way. Storms just happen. Cells in bodies just start multiplying. It's not something that somebody *plans*."

"Molly feels as though her body's turned against her," I said.

"Cancers are just doing what cancers do," said Gwen.

"Then why doesn't God cure her?" asked Pamela.

"Maybe he will," said Liz. "I'm certainly praying for her, and I'm going to ask Father Ryan to say a novena for her too."

I wondered if I went to church more if I'd know more about the power of prayer, but I said, "What I don't understand is that if God knows everything, doesn't he already know about Molly being sick? Doesn't he care for her as much as we do?"

"Of course he does," said Elizabeth.

"Then why do we have to beg him to help her? Why wouldn't he just *do* it? It's like we're trying to get him to change his mind or remind him of what he should be doing."

"I could get in trouble hanging around you, Alice," Liz joked. "You're always asking why."

"I think it's good to ask questions," said Gwen. "Of course, I'd never do it around my grandmother. If I asked her a question like that, she'd pinch my arm black and blue."

We laughed. "Did you ever test her?"

"Just once," Gwen said ruefully. "She was reading us a Bible story about Joshua and his army marching seven times around Jericho, and the walls came tumbling down. The story said they had to destroy the city because it stood in their way to the Promised Land. And I said to my grandmother, 'If they could go *around* it in the first place, why did they have to destroy it? Why didn't they just go around?' She called me 'Miss Smarty-Mouth' and pinched my arm, and my daddy told me later that if I had any more questions about the Bible, I should come to him."

"So did you ask him about Joshua and Jericho?" Liz asked.

"He didn't know either," said Gwen. "He said

that the way men fight today doesn't make any more sense than the way they did back then."

"Smart man," I said. "But right now I'm down on guys." I'd already told them about Brian sending the quiz to Amy. "All I can think about is how to get even with Brian. Amy's been getting e-mails from guys, and so have I. Some guy who was in my Algebra II class last year e-mailed me and said, 'I heard you want to try oral. I'm up for it, if you know what I mean.' I want revenge."

"Problem is, if you gave Brian a quiz like that, he'd *love* for you to publicize his answers," Gwen said. "If he had sex with seventeen girls, he'd want everyone to know it." She was idly turning the pages of the newspaper, her bare feet curled around her can of 7UP on our coffee table.

"What would embarrass Brian would be to say he *wasn't* getting any sex," said Pamela.

"And how would we prove *that*?" I asked.

We went on talking about a punishment to fit his crime, and nothing seemed bad enough for Brian Brewster.

Suddenly Gwen stopped turning pages. "Hey!" she said.

We stopped talking and looked her way. "Look!" she said, and turned the paper around to show us a quarter-page ad for air conditioners.

I didn't get it. There was a picture of a heavy

man hunched over a computer. He wasn't very attractive. His belly hung out over his belt, sweat poured down his face, and he was staring—leering, actually—at a picture of an iceberg in a cold blue ocean on his screen.

The ad read: *Some people settle for fantasy.* And at the bottom of the ad it read, *Why wait? All air conditioners half price,* and gave the details.

"Yeah?" said Pamela.

"We cut off the words at the bottom," said Gwen. "We blank out the picture of the iceberg on his screen and substitute the word 'sex' in big letters. And we print 'Brian Brewster' on the man's T-shirt."

I began to get the picture. "So under the title 'Some people settle for fantasy,' we have a cartoon of Brian getting his kicks by computer instead of the real thing," I said. "Gwen, you are a total *genius!*"

"Pure luck," said Gwen.

"The minute he sees it, he'll tear it up," said Liz.

"Not if we scan it into the computer and send it out as an attachment to every single e-mail address we know," said Gwen. "Someone started circulating that list of e-mail addresses around just before school let out, remember? In the cafeteria? That's probably how Brian got Amy's address; she added hers to the list."

Gwen was the only one of us with a scanner, I had Dad's car for the evening, and you never saw four girls abandon a house as fast as we did, newspaper in hand, heading for Gwen's. We cut and pasted and printed and adjusted. The man in the advertisement even looked a little like Brian. We darkened his hair a little and made his eyebrows a little heavier. And when the cartoon came on the screen, we screamed with delight. Perfect. The absolute perfect revenge.

There was a leering Brian Brewster, his eyes bugging out with pleasure, sweat pouring down his face, staring at the word *SEX* on his computer screen. *Some people settle for fantasy,* it read. We sent it to every address on the list—friends at school and even friends of friends.

Gwen heard back from at least seven girls who said they had received Brian's quiz, three of whom had fallen for it. But we didn't hear from Brian. Keeno told us later that he asked him if he'd gotten the cartoon. Brian said he didn't know what Keeno was talking about, but his ears turned two shades of pink and he'd changed the subject.

10

Families

I was off work on Monday and had spent the morning going through old magazines to clear off some of the shelves in my room—all those supposedly hip magazines for teen girls that I'd bought or that friends had given me, with articles earmarked that I just *had* to read: "See If Guys Find Your Style Fab or Freaky"; "Make Him Wanna Do the Tongue Tango with You"; "What's Your Holiday Groove?" I wonder sometimes if I'm the only one in the state of Maryland who feels that all this stuff was meant for somebody else.

Who writes these articles, anyway? Who says things like, *If your 'rents are having a party at their crib and you're stuck there, wear duds your folks will dig but that are still hot and hip* or *Does your hunk meet your cutie requirements, or is he barf bait who will diss you when he gets a chance?* I mean, who talks like that? None of my friends, that's for sure.

These writers may be thirty-year-old women trying to sound thirteen, but they sound more like what you'd hear if you pressed a button on a Barbie doll.

I found myself chucking magazine after magazine. Maybe I was just growing up faster than I'd thought. Maybe that's why this stuff sounded so juvenile. But I'll admit that the photos of models in swimsuits made me wonder how *I'd* look at the beach, so I spent the afternoon trying on shorts to see which ones I should take with me to Rehoboth. I'd gained a pound and a half last year, but it looked good on me. My arms were slimmer, but my butt had filled out a little, and that was okay with me.

Too bad there isn't a way to lift a pound and a half off one part of your body and put it somewhere else—any place you choose—like the way you can doctor a photo on the computer. I'd take a pound off my stomach and put it on my calves to give my legs a little more shape.

Now, turning around in front of the mirror, my butt did look a little more "pat-able," as Pamela would say. I smiled to myself.

The phone rang and I answered. It was Mrs. Price, Elizabeth's mom.

"Alice, are you working today?" she asked, sounding stressed.

"No, I'm off. Anything wrong?"

"Elizabeth won't be home until four, and I'm supposed to pick Fred up at the airport in an hour. But Nathan's getting over an ear infection, and he's been so miserable and fussy. He fell asleep on his rug about twenty minutes ago, and I'd hate like anything to wake him and put him in the car. I was wondering if you could possibly come over and keep an eye on things till I get back. Name your price."

"I'll do it for nothing," I said. "I've got three books yet to read on my summer reading list, and I'll bring one along."

"Oh, *would* you? Nathan might sleep the whole time. I hope so, anyway," she said.

I slipped my sandals on, ran a brush through my hair, and headed across the street to the Prices' house with *To Kill a Mockingbird* under my arm. Dad was at work, and Sylvia had gone to play tennis. Her car was still out front, though, so I figured she must have gotten a ride with someone.

Mrs. Price was standing at the door holding her car keys. "If he wakes up, he's already had his medicine, so you don't need to give him anything but juice and crackers. Here's my cell phone number."

"We'll be fine," I said.

Elizabeth's house is a lot different from ours. More formal. Mauve drapes are caught up in big gathers and folds above the picture window in the living room, and there's an Oriental rug on the floor. There used to be figurines on the Queen Anne coffee table, but now, I noticed, there was nothing that an almost three-year-old couldn't touch. A plastic truck with rubber wheels lay on its side by the fireplace beside a stuffed dog stuck in an orange juice container.

I settled down in a big wing chair with my book and concentrated on Atticus Finch and his daughter, Scout. I'd read two chapters before I heard the stairs creak and looked up to see Nathan coming down one step at a time, both hands holding on to the railing. He stopped when he saw me.

"Hi, Nathan!" I said, putting down my book. "I came over to play with you!"

He wasn't impressed. "Where's my mommy?" he asked.

"She's gone to get your daddy at the airport. They'll be back soon." I held out my arms. "Come sit on my lap and we'll read a story."

Nathan shook his head, and his lips turned down.

I got up and walked toward the hall. But then I ducked behind the wall to the foyer and called softly, "Na-than!" I peeped out and saw him staring. He smiled when he saw me, then clouded up again.

I moved back through the dining room into the kitchen and peeped out from the wall back there. "Na-than!" I called again, our favorite game whenever I came over. This time I heard him giggle. He padded quickly down the stairs and ran down the hall toward the kitchen, hitting at me when he found me. I swooped him up in my arms and flubbered him on the neck.

"Should we play with your trucks?" I asked.

"No," said Nathan.

"How about if we build a tower with your blocks?"

He shook his head.

I sat down on the couch again with Nathan on my lap, his head heavy against my chest. I picked up a book that was lying nearby, *Angus and the Cat*. It was a well-worn book, probably Elizabeth's when she was small and possibly her mother's before that. It looked old-fashioned and vaguely familiar, as though I could remember myself sitting on somebody's lap, my head against somebody's chest.

Yes, there was the picture of the Scottie dog jumping into a pond after a frog . . . Angus puzzling over a balloon . . . and then . . . the awful day when Angus finds a cat in *his house*.

Nathan sat as though hypnotized, listening to the story, arms and legs motionless. All the while

I tried to connect this story, this book, with someone in my mind. Was it Mother? Aunt Sally? When
we got to the end—*Angus was GLAD the cat came
back!*—I realized that it had been Uncle Milt who
had read that book to me so long ago. And I felt
that regret again that we were clear out here in
Maryland, away from relatives.

We read the book twice, then another book,
then we made a tunnel for Nathan's trucks out of
a set of encyclopedias. When Mr. and Mrs. Price
came in at last, Nathan had on a fresh diaper,
crumbs on his chin, and was helping me blow
soap bubbles in the kitchen.

"Hey, buddy!" his dad called, and Nathan slid
off the chair and ran pell-mell down the hallway to
greet him.

"Alice, thank you *so* much!" Mrs. Price said.
"Please let me pay you."

"Not a chance. Nathan and I had some serious
playtime coming," I said.

As I went outside, I was remembering when
Nathan was born, how I waited with Liz in the
hospital waiting room while her dad was in with
her mom. I smiled as I remembered how we tried
to figure out how a baby could come out of a
woman—reassure ourselves that our bodies
would stretch.

I'd just reached the bottom step of Elizabeth's

porch when I saw a car pull up outside our house. My jaw dropped when I saw Jim Sorringer in the driver's seat. *Sylvia's old boyfriend!* Our vice principal back in junior high school. *Still* the vice principal where Sylvia was teaching.

I slowly put my right foot back on the step and froze as the passenger-side door opened and Sylvia got out with her tennis racket. She leaned down and said something to Jim through the window, and then he drove away.

I felt I couldn't go inside our house just then, and I sat down on the Prices' steps. I had to make sense of what I'd seen. If I walked in now and asked Sylvia about it, it might look as though I'd been spying on her. I stayed for five minutes, then slowly crossed the street.

When I opened our front door, I could hear the shower going upstairs, and after a while Sylvia came down in her cotton robe, a towel around her hair.

"Oh, hi, Alice," she said. "I just got in from tennis. Got a ride both ways." And she went to the back door, opened it, then took the towel off her head. "I think I'll just let my hair dry naturally and to heck with the blow-dryer. It's too hot to put all that heat on my head," she told me.

Was she just going to pretend she hadn't been out with Jim Sorringer? Those weekly sessions

she'd been having on Monday afternoons may not
have been tennis at all. My mind was racing so far
ahead with possibilities that it took my breath
away. I didn't even respond. I took *To Kill a
Mockingbird* up to my room and closed the door.

Sometimes it seems like half the grown-ups
you know are divorced, but I guess that's the
national average. Pamela's folks are divorced
now. My cousin Carol is divorced. Karen's mom
is divorced. Sylvia's sister is divorced. Sam's folks
are separated.

I felt like getting online and asking all my friends
to keep an eye on Sylvia. In fact, I wanted to ask
someone to follow her next Monday and see
where she went. I wouldn't let her get away with
carrying on an affair right under Dad's nose. *Stop
it!* I told myself, but my mind wouldn't listen.

Dad worked till six thirty, and Sylvia asked if I
wanted to eat without him or wait, and I said I'd
wait. I was going to look for signs. Listen for innu-
endos. They say that divorce always comes as a
shock to kids, even when their folks have been
fighting a lot. Dad and Sylvia had been married
only ten months and I hardly ever heard them
argue. But I remembered that kiss Jim Sorringer
had given her at the wedding . . . the way he had
held back till the end of the receiving line. . . .

Dad came in, and Sylvia put dinner on the table.

"Yum. Salmon," he said, and we sat down. As Sylvia passed the salad, she said, "Guess who's engaged."

"Engaged? Your friend Lois?" Dad guessed.

"No."

"Your sister?"

Sylvia laughed. "If only. No, Jim Sorringer."

I dropped my fork and quickly picked it up again.

"To whom?" Dad asked.

"The P.E. teacher at school. The new one we got last year."

"How did you find out?" Dad asked.

"Connie and I were supposed to play doubles with Julie and Ed, but Ed was sick, so they asked Jim to fill in. They beat us, of course, but at least I got some exercise. Connie drove me over, and Jim drove me home. He seems almost giddy with happiness."

"Good match, do you think?"

"I think so. I've seen them around school together, and they look absolutely devoted to each other," Sylvia said.

Did I only imagine it, I wondered, or was that relief on Dad's face? There was certainly relief on mine.

"Don't worry, we won't have to go to the wedding," Sylvia teased. "They're getting married in Iowa, where her parents live."

"Darn," said Dad, holding back a smile.

I told Sylvia I'd do the dishes and clean up the kitchen. After all my unkind thoughts about her, I should have scrubbed the floor as well. That gave them time to look over the sketches Sylvia had made of the new addition.

When you add something new, you give away something old, somebody once told me. I don't know if that's true, but I decided I needed to give up my suspicions about Sylvia and Jim Sorringer. I needed to accept that she loves Dad as much as he loves her.

When I crossed the living room later to go up and get ready for Mark's, I looked at Dad in his armchair and said, "Do you remember reading to me when I was little?"

"Sure," he said. "We read a lot."

"Do you remember a book called *Angus and the Cat*?"

"Hmmm. Seems familiar."

"Did Uncle Milt read to me?"

"Yes. Sally, too. Carol read to you, and even Lester read some. And Grandpa McKinley used to sit you on his knee and read. He liked reading *Huckleberry Finn*, but you were too young for that and slid off every time."

There *had* been family around me once, I thought, when we lived in Illinois. Grandpa

McKinley and my uncles in Tennessee used to come up to visit. There *had* been a time we had uncles and aunts and grandparents around us. It was just that I wanted them *now*, and that wasn't about to happen.

Sometimes I had the feeling that *our* family reunion was still waiting to happen. If not at Les and Tracy's wedding, then some relative could call and organize something else, maybe. My cousin Carol could announce her engagement to somebody. Aunt Marge—the one who married my Uncle Charlie two days before he died on their honeymoon—could marry again. Maybe Sylvia's sister down in Albuquerque could buy a house and invite everyone to a housewarming. Or Sylvia's brother in Seattle could give a college graduation party for his daughter. With relatives, anything could happen.

11

Sad

One thing I learned from working in a department store: I didn't want a job where the highlight of the day was going home and time off was the only thing that mattered. The hours at Hecht's seemed to drag along, and the only bright spots were days like this Monday, when I wasn't working. Whatever contribution I was making to the state of the world was only a drop in the bucket.

Patrick doesn't seem to worry about being a drop in the bucket, though. He's too busy to worry. Too busy to come by every week and join the gang. But on this particular Monday he was there at Mark's when I arrived, and I joined him and Gwen at the umbrella table by the pool. Gwen was telling him how Molly was sort of an epiphany for her.

"How so?" he asked.

"My grandmother would say it was God working

through Molly, but I say it's just Molly, plain and simple, that did it for me."

"Did what?" I asked, sitting down with my Coke.

"Helped me make up my mind to go into medicine for real. That and my internship at NIH," she said.

"It's a long haul, Gwen—medical school," Patrick cautioned.

"You know it! But working in hematology this summer . . . realizing all the diagnostic stuff you can do with blood . . . I don't know. I see kids come into the clinic for chemo—kids a lot sicker than Molly—and I think, 'Yes! This is where I belong.' I'm making friends with some of the doctors. They'll help me figure out how to go about getting into medical school."

She looked at Patrick, who was turning his glass around and around on the tabletop. "How about you?"

"I'm going to major in international relations. Maybe work overseas."

"A diplomat like your dad?" I asked.

"Not that. More a hands-on job. I'll see how it goes."

I always feel so . . . immature, in a way, when either Patrick or Gwen talk about the future. Patrick's starting college a year sooner than the rest of us; Gwen's got an internship with a national agency. . . . What was I doing to prepare myself for a job in psychology? Fastening buttons at Hecht's.

I raised my head and sniffed the air. There was that burning-rope smell I'd noticed the last time we were here at Mark's. I glanced around and figured it was coming from the direction of Brian and Keeno at the far end of the pool. They were sitting on the edge, their legs in the water, smoking . . . something. Mark went over and kidded around a little with Keeno. Took something from him and inhaled, then handed it back.

"They're at it again," I said. Brian had that sleepy, faraway look on his face. Keeno looked a little more nervous, keyed up. I could hardly stand to look at Brian anymore, but not because of this. Because of that sex quiz, I imagined he could see right through me, and his smile always seemed a leer. Yet I had to act friendly and breezy or else he'd know it had really gotten to me. But the fact that he'd tricked Amy and those other girls—the fire in my gut flared again.

"What do you suppose it's like?" I asked.

"Pot?" said Patrick.

"Altered state of consciousness," said Gwen. "Supposed to make you euphoric, relaxed, et cetera."

"Depends how much you smoke," said Patrick.

"You've tried it?" I asked.

"Once," he answered.

I'd asked the question, but I didn't expect the answer. I turned and looked at Patrick. *Patrick!* I was sitting here with maybe two of the smartest kids in the whole school, and one had had sex and one had smoked pot.

"Why?" I asked.

"Because I wanted to see for myself what it was all about."

"So have you tried crack just to see what it's about?"

"I said I was curious, not crazy."

"So what's it like?"

"An everything's-right-with-the-world kind of feeling, I guess. Mellow . . ."

"Then why aren't you sitting down there with Brian?"

"Because I don't trust an artificial high," said Patrick. "Know what I mean?"

"Well, obviously, Brian doesn't go by that philosophy," said Gwen. "We've got a study going about marijuana and its effects on oxygen in the blood, and—"

She stopped talking when the patio door opened and Mrs. Stedmeister came out. We hardly ever saw Mark's parents. It was as though they turned the backyard and pool and family room completely over to Mark's friends when we came—happy to have us there. If we saw them at all, it was usually just to dart in or out like chipmunks, taking empty glasses back into the house or setting out a fresh bowl of chips.

But this time Mrs. Stedmeister stood erect there on the patio, a tall, thin woman with an angular face. She was wearing a pink polo shirt, a beige skirt, and sneakers, her short salt-and-pepper hair like a cap on her head.

"Could I have your attention for a moment?" she said. She was standing beside the table where Patrick and Gwen and I were sitting. When the chatter didn't subside, Patrick picked up a spoon and tapped it on the side of his glass. People turned around and stared.

Now that all eyes were on Mrs. Stedmeister, she appeared self-conscious and cleared her throat twice before she spoke: "Just so you know, there is to be no marijuana smoking at this address, inside or out," she said. It sounded as though she was reciting a speech she had practiced a number of times. "There is also to be no alcohol. If you bring any of these things with you, we'll have to ask you to leave. Thank you."

Mark's face went the color of a peach. He gave an embarrassed smile to Brian, who was discreetly stamping out his joint on the concrete deck. Keeno's fingers closed around the can next to his thigh and slid it behind him. Without further explanation, Mrs. Stedmeister turned and went back inside the house.

We looked around uncomfortably at each other.

"The Pool Nazi has spoken," Mark murmured, but Liz rose to his mom's defense.

"Hey, Mark, she's let us hang out here all these years. Give her a break," she said.

"Damn," murmured Brian. "Let's go to the park. C'mon. Who wants to go to Wheaton?"

"It closes at dusk, Brian," Patrick told him.

"Trust me. I know where to get in," Brian said.

"And they patrol it," Liz reminded him.

"We just have to stay one step ahead of the patrol. No big deal," said Keeno.

"I'm fine here," said Gwen.

Karen made a face. "Oh, c'mon."

"I don't think so," I said.

"Old Play-by-the-Rules McKinley," said Brian, laughing at me.

I could hardly stand him. "You've got that right," I said, and turned away.

The group broke up soon after that. Jill and Justin drove Karen and Penny home. Gwen was spending the night at Yolanda's, and Patrick had an early-morning landscape job. Pamela and Liz and I talked awhile at the corner, then each went to her own house. I thought about Brian and Keeno heading for Wheaton Regional Park in Brian's car. About Yolanda's superstition that someone I knew would die. Somewhere down the line, I figured, if it wasn't Molly, it might be Brian or Keeno, and we'd be putting teddy bears and flowers at some particular place along a highway.

It was almost ten thirty when I started up the walk, and I startled when I saw someone there on the porch. A man. I came to a dead stop, afraid to go on, trying to make out who it was in the darkness. Keeno? Brian? *Patrick?* I took a few more steps. Wrong on all counts. It was Lester.

"Les!" I said, and started up the steps.

"Just leaving," he told me.

"So what's up?" I asked. "Sit down!" I tugged at his arm and pulled him down on the steps beside me.

"I dropped by to see Dad, but he and Sylvia have already sacked up. I hadn't realized it was after ten," he said.

"So talk to *me*!" I said. "It's glorious out."

He hesitated, like I was a poor substitute for Dad, but then he leaned forward and rested his arms on his knees.

"Any news?" I asked hopefully. "Doesn't Tracy have a birthday about now?"

"Yesterday," said Les.

I grinned. "Was she wearing a red or yellow dress?" I asked knowingly. And then I couldn't help myself: "She was at Hecht's looking for a dress for a special occasion."

"That must have been the birthday party her family threw for her the day before. I took her out last night."

I grabbed his arm and shook it. "And? And? Did you buy the ring?"

"She said no."

The words didn't make sense. "She doesn't want a ring?"

"No to getting married, Al. She said it very nicely, of course. But it's still a no."

I could only stare. *"Why?"*

All I could see of Lester's face was the side illuminated by the streetlight. But in that one side I saw such sadness that I could hardly bear it.

"Why, Lester?" I asked again.

He shook his head. "The more she tried to explain it, the more complicated it got, and the more I knew it was over. What it boils down to, I think, is that her family just didn't approve."

"How could they not like you?" I asked, stunned.

"Without much difficulty, it seems."

"But what reason . . . ?"

"Actually, to be fair to them, it wasn't me as much as the idea of marrying outside their race. From what I gather, the strongest objections came from her father and grandmother. The grandmother said that I would never really fit in with that big family—their traditions, their inside jokes, the way they worship. . . . That I would never really feel a part of that."

"Wouldn't that be for you to decide?" I said indignantly. "How does Sylvia fit into ours? How does any outsider get to feeling at home in a family?"

"Yeah. I gave that speech too. But her dad told her I'd just be using her. Either I was attracted to her because I think she's exotic or I'd be using her for political purposes."

"You're running for mayor now?" I asked sarcastically, angry at Tracy's dad. "This is all so insulting to Tracy—that you just find her 'exotic.'"

"I told her that. I asked if I could talk to her dad one-on-one. She said he wouldn't agree to that."

"And how does *she* feel about all this, Les? Isn't that what matters?"

He sighed. "I pulled out all the stops, believe me, but she's afraid it just wouldn't work. It's not that she thinks her dad is right. She says when you marry, it's not just one person: You're marrying a family. It would be me against all sixty-seven of her relatives, and though she's sure they'd always be polite to me, they'd never really look at me as anything but an outsider. And that would break her heart—feeling like she had to choose between them and me."

"But *she's* breaking *yours!* Doesn't she even care about that?" I cried.

Lester didn't answer. I heard him swallow.

"Oh, Les, I'm so sorry!" I said. "I'm mad, too, but I'm really sorry. I liked Tracy a lot."

"Me too," said Les.

"Come on in and I'll make you a shake. Coffee? An omelet? Anything?"

"No, they'd hear us poking around, and if they came downstairs and I spilled my guts, they probably wouldn't sleep very well. I shouldn't have come over this late."

"I'm glad you did. I'm glad you told me."

"Well . . ." He stood up. "I've got to get to bed too, and so do you. I'll let you tell Dad and Sylvia in the morning. I'm too depressed to talk about it anymore."

"Les . . . you'll be okay, won't you?" I asked.

He gave me a weak smile. "I'm not going to jump off a bridge, if that's what you're thinking. 'Night, Al."

He went down the sidewalk, got in his car, and drove away.

*   *   *

They're prejudiced! That's all I could think. *They don't even know Lester. They don't know our family.* Tracy should have stood up for him, defended him!

I couldn't tell anyone before about Lester proposing, and now that he'd been refused, I couldn't tell anyone after. Only Dad and Sylvia, and for that I had to wait till breakfast. Lester had actually confided in me! He'd told me before he'd told Dad, and I felt as incredibly grown up as I felt incredibly sad.

"Oh, I feel so terrible for Les," Sylvia said the next morning, pushing her roll away.

Dad silently sipped his coffee.

"It's prejudice, Dad! If he were black, they wouldn't be talking this way about him not fitting in, as though that's the only thing to consider. So he wouldn't know their family jokes! Big deal! They'd explain them to him! That's what families do. They just don't want Tracy to marry a Caucasian, and they won't make the effort to get to know Lester as a person. How could she let her family decide something that important for her?"

"There's another possibility," Dad said.

"What?"

He shrugged. "Maybe Tracy wasn't that much in love with him to begin with."

I looked at him incredulously. Not in love with

Lester? How could any woman not love my brother? Marilyn and Crystal used to be crazy about him! "Then why did she go out with him all those months?" I wanted to know.

"Why does anyone go out with someone? Because she was trying to get to know him better—see how she felt."

I thought of all the times I'd seen them together. It had always been Les who was doing the hand-holding, the back-of-the-neck massaging, the brushing together of the lips—all the little gestures you make when you're in love. Hadn't I wondered about it then? That they never seemed to originate with Tracy?

"Then . . . maybe Les just jumped the gun and proposed too soon! Maybe if Tracy's family gets to know him better—," I said.

"Al, keep out of it. My guess is that her answer is pretty final. If it's not, she'll let him know," Dad said.

I just couldn't believe it. I'd been so *sure*. I hadn't even considered the possibility that Tracy might not love him enough, and then I was surprised at myself for *not* considering it.

What had turned her off? I wondered. What didn't she like about Lester? The way he walked? Talked? Smelled? Ate? Laughed? Joked? Kissed? His haircut? His taste in music? Clothes? Beer? Was it religion? Values? Somehow Tracy just didn't see him fitting into that close-knit family of hers, and I'd lost the sister I'd never had. I was more devastated than I had any right to be, because deep down, deeper than I'd even dug before, I wondered if I hadn't thought that Tracy would be thrilled to marry a Caucasian. Flattered that he loved her. Eager to get involved in our family. And perhaps, all this time, it was Les who didn't quite measure up.

What were *our* family traditions? What were *our* inside jokes? How did our Christmas rituals start? Was there ever a round-robin letter that went from family to family? What stories or heirlooms were passed down from generation to generation? Quilts? Silver? *Anything?* If there was a quiz called "Family," would we even pass?

I hunkered down in my chair. "I'm still upset with her," I murmured. "Some people wouldn't know a good thing if it fell in their laps."

Suddenly Dad started to chuckle. "You sound just like your mother, Alice. That's just what Marie used to say and the way she said it."

It was Gwen who asked. Not about an engagement. Just whether Les and Tracy were still an item.

"I don't think so," I said.

"Really? Any idea why?"

I shrugged. "I think maybe he liked her more than she liked him. It's just a guess."

"Probably the grandmother," said Gwen.

"What?"

"When a grandmother makes up her mind, you've got a mountain to climb in order to change it."

"What can we do to change Tracy's grandmother?" I asked.

"Change four hundred years of black history," said Gwen.

So here's where things stood with what was left of the summer: Les and Tracy were kaput; Jim Sorringer was engaged; Molly was going through chemo; Faith had definitely given up her scumbag ex-boyfriend for Chris; Mrs. Stedmeister had put her foot down about marijuana and beer in her backyard; and Liz and Pamela and I were packing to go to the beach with Pamela's dad.

I told Juanita at Hecht's that I'd be back on August 23, and I found a new bathing suit on sale. The day we left, Mr. Price drove Liz and me over to the Joneses', and Liz and Pam and I sat out on the front steps as Pamela's dad packed the minivan.

I saw there was room for one more and wished

Pamela had invited Gwen, but of course she couldn't. Her dad had told her once that if she ever brought home a black boyfriend, he wouldn't let either one of them in the house. The same was probably true for girlfriends.

Just then, however, a green Honda pulled up in front, and a woman stepped out carrying a large bag in one hand, a smaller case in the other.

I stared. "Meredith?" I asked.

"She's coming too?" asked Liz.

"Apparently," said Pamela. "Dad probably didn't tell me because he didn't want Mom to know."

"What's to know?" I asked. "Your mom could date again if she wanted."

"It doesn't quite work that way," said Pamela. "I think Mom figures that as long as Dad doesn't marry again, she still has a chance with him. I haven't seen a ring yet, but if Dad and Meredith are engaged, I don't want to be the one to tell Mom."

"You know what?" I told them as we watched Mr. Jones and Meredith work to squeeze her bags in the minivan beside ours. "I'm going to go these whole four days without thinking of love once."

"With all the guys around on the beach?" said Pamela. "The tanned bodies, the bleached hair, the furry chests, the thick thighs, the sweaty backs, the—"

"Nope!" I said. "They're all irrelevant. I'm going to enjoy my girlfriends. I'm going to play volleyball and bodysurf and read books and shop and—"

"Watch for hunks out of the corner of your eye," said Pamela.

12

Sun and Sand

It's about three hours from Silver Spring, Maryland, to Rehoboth Beach in Delaware. More, when you count the slow crawl of traffic over the Bay Bridge and the even slower procession into town.

Mr. Jones and Meredith sat in front, Liz and I were in the middle seat, and Pamela sprawled out on the third seat, her legs draped over the cooler and the bags piled at one end. Pamela's dad was very tall. His face was pockmarked from early years of acne, but he was handsome in a rugged kind of way. Meredith was a plain-looking woman who wore her long brown hair flipped up in back, the ends fastened to her head with a clip. If she wore makeup at all, it wasn't noticeable. Nice figure. Healthy-looking, I guess you'd call her.

Mr. Jones consented to put our CDs in the player, but he turned off the speakers up front, I noticed:

Thrill me with your hot lips, baby,
Put your powerful hands upon my thigh.
Let me feel your love inside me, baby,
Hold me till I truly wanna die.

We caught Mr. Jones and Meredith exchanging amused glances, but it didn't keep us from singing along. I can't carry a tune, of course, so I just spoke the words, but Liz and Pamela really cut loose on the refrain:

Baby, baby, baby,
Gimme sweet, sweet kisses,
Baby, baby, baby,
I'm your one-night missus. . . .

I turned toward the window and took in the view. I'd been to the ocean only once that I remembered, but I love the Chesapeake Bay Bridge. As you approach the tollbooth, you can see cars high up there on the curved span, and finally, when it's *you* up there, you look down on a sea of sailboats from a road bridge three hundred feet up and four and a half miles across.

"Did you know that some people panic when they get up here on the bridge?" Meredith said to us over her shoulder. "I had a friend who had to wrap herself in a blanket and curl up on the floor of the backseat before her husband drove them across. She'd whimper the whole time."

We laughed, but then I remembered my old fear of the deep end of swimming pools. I'd probably still be afraid of deep water if Les hadn't helped me through it. I guess everybody's got something. . . .

When we turned off Route 50 and took a back road to the southeast, we drove through small towns that Mr. Jones said were speed traps. We saw lots of American flags. Lots of people sitting on porches, watching the tourists stream through. As we did the homestretch into Rehoboth, Pamela declared she could walk faster than we were traveling. So we entertained ourselves by waving and hooting at cars full of guys who were stuck in traffic beside us, kidding around with them, telling them we were eighteen. One of them asked where we were staying, but Pamela's dad wouldn't give us the address.

And then finally—*finally*—we pulled up to the small yellow cottage that a friend of Mr. Jones had loaned him. It was about three blocks back from the beach and not quite what we had imagined. But it had a screened porch and a grill out back, so it would do. As soon as we were assigned a bedroom, we put on our swimsuits, pulled on our cutoffs and sneakers, grabbed our towels, and took off.

"Freedom!" Liz cried, flinging her arms open

wide, which happened to clip a guy right in the mouth as he was walking around us on the sidewalk.

"Oh God, I'm so sorry!" she said, but he just grinned and went on. That put us in a good mood—that you could accidentally clip someone in the mouth and he wouldn't get mad.

Everything smells different at the ocean. The air smells of fries, fudge, fish, and coconut oil lotion. Everything feels different—wet sand underfoot, the heat of the boardwalk, the breeze in the face. Things sound different—the continual shriek of gulls, the laughter of children, the music coming from the shops, the soft wallop of breakers on the beach.

Guys looked down on us from motel balconies as we walked along the boardwalk, and some of them shouted out party invitations:

"Come by around nine. . . ."

"We'll look for you at ten. . . ."

"Hey! Come and bring your girlfriends. . . ."

We just laughed. Some little kid got separated from her parents and was howling loudly; we stayed with her until her frantic mother came rushing out of a shop and swooped her up in her arms. We bumped into little children carrying balloons, girls with cotton candy. Passed guys with

T-shirts saying I'M WITH STUPID (arrow pointing to a friend) and guys with no T-shirts at all. We bought Pennsylvania Dutch pretzels, ate half, and took the rest down to the water to feed to the gulls.

Pamela wanted to lie on the beach and flirt with the lifeguard, but Sylvia says that the sun wrinkles you—sun and smoking—and I'd rather be in the water anyway. At least you're moving when you're horsing around, not just letting one side of your body, then the other, slowly bake.

I liked sloshing ankle-deep in the foam, trying to pick up little shells before they were washed out to sea again. Liked going in up to my knees, where I could back up when I saw a wave coming. But I was still afraid of the breakers.

Liz wanted to swim out beyond the point where the waves were breaking, so that we could just float around in the gentle rolling of the ocean. But to do that, we had to wade out there, and every fifteen seconds or so, another wave came in. Once you're in waist-deep, you can't jump over them any longer. And if they knock you down, you go head over heels, your knees scraping the sandy bottom, water throbbing in your ears, the force of the water tossing your head first one way, then another. I hate that. I hate water in my nose and ears, which is why I never learned to dive.

We were holding on to each other's arms, and

Liz said, "Alice, you're shaking! Are you cold?"

"I'm—I'm terrified!" I said. "Oh God, here comes another one!"

Here's what girlfriends do. Here's what *real* friends say: "We're going to teach you to go under them," Liz said.

"No!" I cried, horrified at the thought of all that water thundering over me.

"When I say 'duck,' hold your nose and try to sit on the bottom," she yelled.

"I'll die!" I said, my voice quavering.

Pamela just laughed. "Here comes one! Get ready!"

I screamed as I watched the green water swelling higher and higher before me, like an open mouth, ready to swallow me up.

"Now!" shouted Liz, tugging at my arm. "Duck!" She pulled me down. I held my nose, and with her tugging at me from one side, Pamela from the other, I tried to sit on the ocean's bottom. I could hear the rush of water over my head, feel my body sway with the current, but I wasn't swept up in it. And when Pamela and Liz pulled me to my feet again, the water around us was calm.

"It worked!" I said in wonder, wiping the water from my eyes.

"Get ready! Here comes another one!" shouted Liz.

Down we went a second time as the next wave washed over us. All I could hear was a roar. This time I stood up laughing, excited, eager for the next one. It was as though it was me against the ocean, and I had won. It could hiss and roar and throw a tantrum, but I was safe as a snail if I kept to the bottom.

You feel ten feet tall when you do something that had always frightened you before. Between each wave, we hurriedly moved out a little farther, and finally the waves were breaking behind us, and the water ahead of us was calm.

We floated around on our stomachs, then our backs. The lifeguard—a short, stocky guy in red trunks—blew his whistle when we got too near a rocky breakwater, and we had to swim away from it.

"You think I should drift over to the rocks again and make him come get me?" asked Pamela mischievously.

"No. There are riptides," Liz said. "But you could always lie at his feet in the hot sand and have a sunstroke. That would get his attention."

After we'd showered that evening and tried to get every last grain of sand out of our private places, we ate take-out food on the screened porch with Mr. Jones and Meredith. Nobody wanted to cook our first night at the beach. Meredith wanted to watch an Orioles game on TV, so she and Mr. Jones sat on one side of the porch at a card table while we chattered away on the other. We'd planned to spend the rest of the evening on the boardwalk and were hugely disappointed when a steady rain began to fall. We decided to just hang out back in our bedroom and plan what we were going to do the next day.

Once the door closed behind us, though, Pamela said, "I feel weird."

"Weird how?" I asked.

"Dad here with somebody else. I know he deserves a little happiness, and I'll be glad if he marries again, but . . . I don't know. Weird."

"Things happen," I said. "People change. My dad didn't plan on losing my mom. Your dad didn't plan on being single again."

Liz sighed. "How do you ever know what's ahead?"

"I may not get married at all," said Pamela. "I'll be one of those women who's married to her career."

"I want both," I said. "I want two kids—maybe three—and I want to live near Dad and Lester. I want my children to have aunts and uncles and cousins and grandparents coming in and out of the house all the time. At Christmas, I want two dozen people at my table . . . and big picnics on the Fourth of July. I want—"

Somebody's cell phone was ringing, and we dived for our bags to see whose it was. Then we recognized Pamela's ring, which sounds more like an ice-cream truck than a cell phone. She checked the number before she answered. "Mom," she told us. Then, "Hi, Mom," and held the phone away from her ear so Liz and I could hear. I lay back on the bed.

"Hi, Pamela. I just wanted to make sure you got there okay. Traffic bad?" came her mom's voice.

"Horrible," Pamela told her. "It took twenty-five minutes just to get over the Bay Bridge because of the backup."

"You girls having a good time? What all did you do today?"

"Well, it's pouring right now, but it was nice earlier," Pamela said. "We just walked the board-walk awhile and went swimming."

"Well, it will be warm, anyway," Mrs. Jones said. "Mid-eighties, the paper said, and . . ."

Just then Meredith tapped on our door, opened it, and said, "After the rain stops, we're going to turn off the air conditioner and—Oh, I'm sorry. I didn't know you were on the phone."

"Who's that?" came Mrs. Jones's voice over the phone. "Pamela, who was that?"

"I'll come back," Meredith said, and went out again, closing the door behind her.

Pamela fell back on the bed dramatically, letting go of the phone.

"Pamela? . . . Pamela?" came her mother's voice.

She put the phone to her ear again. "The land-lady," she said.

"Pamela, don't lie," said her mom.

"Then don't ask a question that will just get you upset," Pamela said.

"Bill said he was taking you and your friends to the ocean. Did he bring that woman? I can't *believe* he would bring her along in front of you girls."

"Mom!" Pamela said. "They're out on the porch watching a ball game. That's hardly something we can't see. You *are* divorced, you know. You can have friends too."

"What's she like?" asked her mother.

"We're not having this conversation, Mom," Pamela told her.

"I'm just asking a simple question," said Mrs. Jones.

"Well, I don't want to get into this. Have a good night, Mom," Pamela said.

Mrs. Jones sighed. "You're right. I'm sorry! Have a good time."

Pamela pressed END and put down the phone.

The room was quiet a moment. Then she gave a

huge sigh. "You know what?" she said. "I'm tired of playing the parent. It's as though they think *they* have all the problems and I'm living my life just fine. 'We'll dump on Pamela! She'll know what to do.' Well, to hell with that."

"You did a good job, though," I told her. "You handled it well."

Pamela shook her head. "For the rest of this trip I want to be me. Sixteen, not forty-six. I want to sleep and eat and flirt and swim and shop and not have to think about what Mom's doing that I can't tell Dad or what he's doing that I can't tell Mom."

"Okay, let's plan tomorrow," said Liz, and we focused on what we'd wear on the boardwalk.

13

Lost

It was still raining when we woke the next morning, and it was almost too much to bear. We had only three days left, and one of those would be spent driving back to Silver Spring.

Meredith was scrambling eggs for us and put a platter on the table sprinkled with crumbled bacon. "There's a movie theater in town and a bookstore. Lots of little shops. You could try those," she said. I wondered if she'd been here before with Pamela's father.

"The theater would be packed," said Pamela. But we definitely did not want to stay inside all day, so after we'd eaten, we put on the plastic ponchos that hung behind the door and set out, our flip-flops flapping on the sidewalk for three blocks, then on up the ramp to the boardwalk.

The lifeguards must have been in the shops too, because their stations were deserted. A few solitary figures plodded, heads down, along the shoreline. A girl and guy were making out on a bench, holding an umbrella over themselves, but mostly people crowded inside the stores, the arcades, and ran from doorway to doorway to escape the rain.

As the wind picked up, we took refuge under the awning of a fudge shop, where a young guy at the front was spinning pink cotton candy at the open window. He grinned at me as I leaned in out of the rain.

"Great day, huh?"

"Yeah. And we've only got three left," I said.

"Bummer. Where you from?" He was deftly holding a paper cone to the side of a large spinning kettle as finely spun sugary strands stuck to the cone until it reached the size of a melon. Then he set it in a holder, picked up another, and began spinning again.

"Maryland. Silver Spring," I told him.

"Silver Springs, huh?"

"Singular. I don't know why so many people put an 's' on the end. How about you? Where are you from?"

"Jersey. I get a job here every summer."

"How's the pay?" asked Pamela.

"Not as good as waiting tables, but I like the boardwalk. Hangin' out with anyone here?"

"No. Just the three of us," said Liz.

He smiled again. "Well, you'll get a lot of invitations if you do the boardwalk. I mean, guys calling out and stuff."

"Yeah? Any parties we should know about?" asked Pamela, interested, I could tell.

"Margaritaville is a hot one. You can't miss it. They put out a banner and do the whole bit on a balcony—rubber palm trees, pink flamingos, the works. You go to any of these, just be sure to take your drink from a bottle and open it yourself. Don't drink anything from a paper cup—no telling what they put in it."

"Thanks for the tip. I doubt we'll be going to any parties, though," I said.

"Yeah, my dad's along this trip," Pamela said.

"Bummer," the guy said again, and laughed.

Miraculously, the rain turned to a light patter, and the sun was struggling to come through.

"Look at that!" Liz said happily.

"So where do *you* hang out?" Pamela asked the guy.

"Mostly here. My girlfriend works at the sandal shop. Stop in there and tell her Jerry sent you. She'll give you ten percent off."

"Thanks, Jerry," we said. "See you around."

We never made it, though, because Liz spotted the Lucky Lady Saloon, like a movie set, where you

could choose your own costumes and pose however you wanted. The photographer took your picture and produced it in that old-timey sepia shade.

"We've got to do this!" she said, and pointed at
the dozens of photos there on the walls.

At the moment some guys in cowboy costumes,
Jesse James look-alikes, were posing as outlaws
and were having trouble keeping their faces
straight as friends of theirs hooted from the side-
lines. Most of the people who had posed for their
pictures took on the stern, unsmiling faces of
people of long ago, who had to strike a pose and
hold it. The photographer took several shots. The
guys were dripping with perspiration when they
took off their hats and leather chaps.

"C'mon, girls!" the photographer called to us.
"What'll it be? Dazzle your boyfriends! Surprise
your friends! Shock your parents!" The crowd
laughed.

We looked through a book of photos to see what
kind of picture we wanted. We rejected the more
prim and proper dresses with necklines all the way
up to the chin.

"Showgirls," said Liz. "We've got to be barroom
showgirls."

"Hey, dig those black net stockings," I said.

"I want the strapless gown with the corset top,"
said Pamela.

An employee handed us clothes from off a rack. The colors didn't make any difference, because they wouldn't show, but I got a yellow satin with a slit up to *here,* Pamela got a tight-fitting black number with corset ties holding the bosom together, and Liz got a red dress that looked positively stunning on her. Like the saloon facade, these were only tie-on costumes, open in the back. Over our bikini tops and shorts they looked fine from up front, and that's all that mattered. The cowboy guys whistled and carried on, and we really hammed it up for the camera.

I sat on a barstool and crossed my legs, so that the slit revealed everything except my underwear. Pamela leaned back against the bar, holding a long cigarette holder. But Liz decided to pose holding two pistols at hip level and glaring menacingly at the camera. I don't know how we managed not to laugh, but there we were, with rows of fake bottles on the wall behind us. We each bought a print that cost a fortune, but we didn't care. It was worth it.

"Dad'll float us a loan if we need it," Pamela said. "Even he'll get a kick out of this picture."

"Look at your legs, Alice! Sex-y!" said Liz.

"And your boobs, Pamela! You're practically popping out!" I said. "We've got to show these around the next time we go to Mark's."

"I wonder what it would be like to be a real showgirl for a day," Liz mused. "Do you suppose they lead exciting lives, or do they go home and do their laundry like everyone else?"

"Do their laundry like everyone else," I said. "Everybody does laundry, gets zits, gets the flu. . . ."

"So what do we do next?" Liz asked, looking around for possibilities.

"Rent a Jet Ski!" said Pamela. "We absolutely have to ski out on the inlet tomorrow before we leave."

We spent the afternoon in the water, then helped make dinner that night. Mr. Jones really laughed at our photos at the Lucky Lady Saloon.

"Would you look at that pistol-packin' mama!" he said, pointing to Liz. "Pretty or not, I'd hate to meet up with her in a dark alley!"

"This is priceless, Pamela. It's a riot," Meredith said. We thought so too. It was then that we noticed the small diamond on Meredith's finger. I think Pamela and I both saw it at the same time.

"Well, hey!" Pamela said. She looked at Meredith, then at her Dad, who was shucking corn at the sink. "Do you guys have an announcement to make?"

Meredith laughed and looked at Mr. Jones. "We went and did it! We're engaged."

"Congratulations!" we said, and Mr. Jones grinned at us.

"Have you set a date?" Pamela asked them.

"No. We haven't gotten that far yet," said her dad.

It was a festive evening. Mr. Jones boiled the corn, Liz and Pamela and I made a big exotic salad with artichokes and mushrooms and peanuts and stuff, and Meredith fried the crab cakes. I watched her mixing the crabmeat and crumbs and celery and egg whites, forming the mixture into round cakes, and placing them in a hot skillet.

I wasn't too sure how I felt about her yet. How *Pamela* felt about her, which was all that counted. We all wanted the best stepmom we could get for Pamela. If I had to describe Meredith to someone, I would say, *Plain, polite, and to the point,* I guess. And there wasn't anything wrong with that.

"I don't know if you girls want to do any shopping," Meredith said, "but I saw some great widebrimmed straw hats in a shop next to a bicycle rentals place. Ribbons, bands, everything! You might want to check them out. Help keep the sun off your faces."

"Where would we ever wear a wide-brimmed straw hat?" I wondered aloud. "Tea party with the queen?"

"Mark's pool," said Pamela.

"Yeah, at night," said Liz, laughing, and we

decided it was just crazy enough to go for it.

"Well, except for the rain last night, I'd say we've been having fairly decent weather," Mr. Jones commented.

"It's been great," I told him.

"It's been good having you," he said. "I don't think Pamela would have enjoyed rattling around the cottage with just the two of us."

I wondered how a man who could be so friendly to us could be prejudiced against African Americans. How, if what Pamela said was true, he wouldn't let Gwen in their house.

"I'm sure going to miss this breeze," said Meredith. "We don't get much of a breeze in Bethesda around the hospital."

"Where do you work?" I asked her.

"Suburban. Orthopedic ward."

"Isn't that near NIH?" I asked. "We have a friend at school who's doing a student internship there this summer."

"A high school student at the National Institutes of Health? She must be one bright cookie," Meredith said.

"She is! She helps out in the hematology lab. She's brilliant in almost everything. I could never have passed algebra if it wasn't for her."

"Is this one of your friends too, Pam?" Mr. Jones asked.

"Yeah. Gwen roomed with us in New York. She was at camp with us too," Pamela said, and I'll bet anything she'd never shown him the pictures we took.

"Well, maybe some of her smarts will rub off on you," he joked.

"I hope so," said Pamela. "I'll invite her over sometime." Pamela made eye contact with me for a nanosecond before adding, "She's African American and as nice as she is smart."

Mr. Jones stopped chewing for a moment, but he didn't respond. I figured that whatever he was thinking, he wasn't about to say it in front of Liz and me. Maybe he wasn't about to say it in front of Meredith, either. All he said was, "I think I'll have another ear of that corn, Liz, if you'll pass the platter. You girls eat up, now. There's more on the stove."

Was he sitting there wondering how he could retract what he said about Gwen's smarts rubbing off on Pamela? Or was he examining his own prejudice? Had falling in love mellowed him out? It was hard to say.

We did buy some straw hats after dinner—wide-brimmed numbers, the kind movie stars wear when they go to the Riviera. Mine was just a hat rim, actually, with a wide black ribbon around it. Liz had a large filmy ribbon at the back of hers, while Pamela bought one with fringe around the edge. We were spectacular!

We walked the length of the boardwalk, hats in hand, stopping in shops along the way to browse. We even sat in on an auction for a while to watch someone bid on an absolutely awful-looking clock that no one in his right mind would have put on his mantel.

When we finally reached the north end of the boardwalk, we took off our sandals and went down to walk at the water's edge.

It was so still down by the ocean. The music and flashing lights and shouts from back on the boardwalk seemed far away. We maneuvered around jellyfish stranded there on the sand, the tide sloshing safely against our ankles, and put our arms around each other's shoulders, bracing ourselves as we walked with our faces turned up toward the sky. We found the North Star and the Big and Little Dippers before Liz tripped over some driftwood and almost fell down.

As we started on again, I said, "So, Pamela, what do you think?"

"About what?"

"Your new stepmother."

"She's not my stepmother yet. They've been going out for a year and a half and have broken up twice, so a lot can happen," Pamela said.

"She seems nice," Liz told her.

"I guess," said Pamela. "But you know what I'd settle for right now? Just . . . *knowing*. That Dad and Mom's marriage is definitely over and that Meredith and Dad are really going to marry. That Mom's going to stay single and that Dad and Meredith are going to stay married. I just want some kind of family I can *count* on, you know? One way or the other. I don't want 'This is my stepmom' one day and 'No, she's not' the next." And then Pamela said, "You know who my real family is? You guys. Because *you* I can count on."

I ignored the little catch in her voice and gave her waist a playful squeeze. "You mean we can't ever change?"

"Only for the better," said Pamela.

"Of *course* for the better!" said Liz. "We're babes tonight, remember! We're gorgeous!"

"Hey, Silver Springs!" we heard someone yell. It was Jerry, the cotton candy guy, chasing a ball over the sand. "You wanna play?"

We looked over at the volleyball net strung up on the beach under the boardwalk lights, where a half dozen players waited for him.

"C'mon!" he urged us. "I need more on my team."

We went back with him, weighted our hats down with our sandals so they wouldn't blow away, and played. Liz went to the other side of the net to balance things out, and Pamela and I played with Jerry.

Pamela was the best of us three, not that anyone really cared. The one other girl—Jerry's girlfriend, I guess—always said, "Good shot!" when one of us managed to get the ball over the net. We served, we volleyed, we missed, we tumbled and got to our feet again, and when we said good night at last, we were wonderfully tired, covered with sweat and sand, and went into the ocean with all our clothes on just to cool off. It's a wonder Meredith let us in the door when we got back. Even more miraculous that our straw hats made it home, only a little worse for wear.

Mr. Jones drove us to the Jet Ski place on the inlet the next afternoon and said this was his treat. He'd be back at four to pick us up. Our swimsuits were still wet, so we'd put on shorts and long-sleeved shirts to protect us from the sun.

I'd never done this before. The line of Jet Skis and Wave Runners there on the water looked like motorcycles on skis. I was amazed the owners would let us take them out without knowing if we could drive. If we could ride a bicycle, even!

We left our sandals behind, put on the regula-tion life jackets, then waded out in the thigh-deep water where one of the employees was waiting to help us on.

He was a good-looking, thirtyish man in cutoffs, with a dark ponytail and a purple shirt. I was first in line, and he gave me a boost up onto the seat.

"Okay, this is your accelerator," he said. "Be careful when you're making turns not to cut it too sharply. And in case you tumble over"—he fastened a cord to my wrist, the other end attached to the Jet Ski—"you won't be separated from your ski. Be sure to keep thirty feet from everyone else, and head back in forty-five minutes. Now," he said, addressing all three of us, "here are the boundaries. Stay fifty feet from the shoreline at all times, and when you come back, come in through those white markers. Turn off your engine when you get to the first one, and we'll bring you in the rest of the way."

We looked where he was pointing. "See that tall smokestack to the north? Don't go farther than that. To the south"—he turned—"don't go beyond the Lighthouse Restaurant. You can't miss it. You'll see their big sign from the water."

"Got it," I said, excited and a little scared.

Of course I killed the engine the first time I tried, and I could hear Liz and Pamela giggling behind me. But then it caught, and when I got the hang of it, I moved slowly through the white markers and into the bay. Rehoboth Bay is on the other side of the highway from the ocean, a sort of inlet away from the sea.

My face caught the breeze and my hair flew out behind me as I skimmed over the water. A passing Jet Ski left a wake, and as I hit each wave, it thunked hard against my own machine. I instantly slowed to avoid tipping over. But soon I learned to take the waves head-on and went a little faster. *Thunk . . .thunk . . . thunk,* as the engine picked up speed.

I saw Liz waving at me on my right and slowed to hear what she was calling.

"What do we do if we run out of gas?" she yelled.

"Who knows?" I answered, and daringly added, "Who cares?" and sped away, laughing.

This was fantastic.

For a while we sort of hung out together, thirty feet apart. But we couldn't really talk above the roar of the engines, and pretty soon we were each going our own way, testing to see how fast we dared go, watching the other skiers cavorting about on the water.

I hadn't realized that the inlet was so immense. From out in the middle, the trees and houses back on land looked small and indistinct. The boundaries we'd been given gave us more room than I'd thought, and there was a long distance, it seemed, between the smokestack in one direction and the Lighthouse Restaurant in the other.

Two younger boys were horsing around too close to each other for comfort, and a man with a child on the seat behind him rode by and bawled them out. But other than that—that and the noise of the Jet Skis—it was a solitary time there on the water. Now and then Liz or Pamela would come into view and we'd grin and wave, but then we'd be off again on our own—*thunk . . . thunk . . . thunk*—our hair streaming out behind us. It was great!

I realized with a pang that I had hardly thought of Lester once. Here I was having a marvelous time at the ocean, and Lester—who'd thought that a life with Tracy stretched out before him—didn't have anything more to look forward to than another evening at home with his roommates. Another week of looking after old Mr. Watts in the rooms below. Another paper to write for graduate school.

I felt I should be there. Should have called him. Should be baking brownies for him—anything to cheer him up. And as much as I wished my time at the ocean could go on forever, I was suddenly glad that we were leaving the next day.

I glanced at my watch and saw that forty minutes had gone by more quickly than I'd realized. Five more minutes and it would be time to head back. I decided to go all the way to the chimneys again, then all the way to the restaurant, before I took my Jet Ski back in, going as fast as I dared. I didn't want anyone calling me a wimp.

Accelerating faster and faster, I could feel the buzz of vibration in the palms of my hands where I gripped the handlebars. The vibration in the seat.

"Whee!" I yelled to the wind, my white shirt flapping wildly as I tilted the Jet Ski into a curve at the southern boundary and headed north again.

Okay, so I'd stayed out a little longer than forty-five minutes, but there would undoubtedly be a line of machines near the shore waiting for the attendant to come and bring us all in.

I looked toward the beach for Jet Skis, but I didn't know exactly where to look. Somehow I thought I'd clearly see the drop-off location, but the shoreline was long, people were small, and I realized, with a jolt, that I had no idea what the Jet Ski place looked like from the water.

I couldn't remember if the office was a building or a shed. Whether there was a sign, a flag, a pole, a wharf . . . I had taken my ski right out into the inlet without looking back and had no idea in this world where I was. My heart began to pound.

Sometimes when I'm scared, I talk out loud to

myself like a grown-up. "Okay, Alice," I said. "Calm down. Now *think*! Where did you take your shoes off? Where did you leave your bag? Was it inside or out? Was there a big sign in the parking lot? *Was* there a parking lot?"

And aloud I answered, "I don't know! I don't know!" I had been so excited about going in the first place that I hadn't noticed anything else around me, only the Jet Skis and the water.

"Okay, look for those white markers," I told myself. But that was useless. They weren't a tenth the size of a Jet Ski, and I couldn't even see any of those.

"Go in closer and just start checking the shoreline," I told myself. "It's got to be about halfway between the chimneys and the restaurant." Or was it? Maybe it was a lot closer to one boundary than the other. I hadn't noticed that, either.

What if I ran out of gas? What if everyone was back but me, and I was left bobbing about on the water?

I looked at my watch again. I should have been back ten minutes ago. I wondered if the engine wasn't beginning to sound funny. Maybe it was low on gas already! I slowed down to save the gas I had, but I slowed too much and killed the engine.

The silence terrified me. "Help!" I bleated to the wind.

I got it started again, but I didn't feed it enough gas and again it died. When I started it a third time, it caught, and I moved slowly along, scanning the shoreline, looking desperately for any sign of Liz or Pamela.

Fifteen minutes late now. Surely *some*one would miss me. Would they charge us extra—figure I'd just decided to go for two rides instead of one? Had everyone else found their way back but me? Was I the only idiot in the bunch?

And then I did run out of gas. Or something. At least, the engine sputtered, sputtered once again, and died. The water was absolutely still. The only sound was the gentle slapping of water against the side of the Jet Ski as it rocked gently to and fro.

"Help!" I whimpered again pitifully. Someone, somewhere, should be watching. Maybe if I took off my shirt, I thought, and waved it above my head, someone would see. Someone would call 9-1-1 and send a helicopter or something.

Maybe the Jet Ski place closed down at four and everyone was leaving. Maybe there was an ordinance about noise after four o'clock.

Frantically, I unbuttoned my shirt, slipped it off, and waved it back and forth in the air.

"Help!" I wept. "Somebody be watching, please!"

What if I was out here all night? I could see the headline: SILVER SPRING GIRL DISAPPEARS AT REHOBOTH AFTER JET SKI DISASTER.

There was a faraway noise, and I recognized the sound of a Jet Ski. I squinted out over the water and, far down the bay, saw one coming toward me, bumping and bobbing over the water. I put my shirt back on.

It was the man with the ponytail. I couldn't see his face well enough to know if he was angry or not. Finally he pulled up beside me.

"Trouble?" he asked.

"I thought I'd be here all night," I said in a small voice. "I think I've run out of gas."

"I doubt that, but we've had a little trouble with that one," he said.

I stared at him. They'd had trouble with this one, yet they'd sent me out on it? But you don't bite the hand of a man who has come to rescue you, so I kept my comments to myself. He was trying not to laugh, though, I could tell.

"I thought maybe if I waited long enough, you'd take off your shorts too," he said.

"You *saw*?" I cried.

He laughed. "My partner had his binoculars out, trying to find you. He said there was some girl out here taking off her clothes."

"I didn't know what else to do," I said.

"Here," he told me, holding my Jet Ski steady. "Climb on behind me."

I grabbed hold of his muscled arm and swung one leg over the seat. He skillfully tied a cable from his Jet Ski to mine, and then we took off, me holding tightly to his waist, his ponytail flapping in my face, hydroplaning over the water, the spray splashing up on our legs.

Everyone was waiting for us when we pulled in. Liz and Pamela were bent over laughing.

"They said you were out there doing a striptease!" Liz said into my shoulder as they pulled me up the bank.

"Everyone wanted a chance with the binoculars," Pamela added, giggling.

"I was terrified!" I said, laughing a little too. "I didn't know what else to do."

I found my sandals and saw Mr. Jones waiting for us in the parking lot. I took a look around me. Yes, there was a big sign. Yes, there was a small white building with a red roof. I should have noticed all this before.

As we walked by the attendants, the one with the binoculars murmured, "Hey, nice bra!"

14

Living Dangerously

That evening, our last night at the ocean, we went to a seafood restaurant with Meredith and Pamela's dad. Liz and Pamela and I paid for their dinner, and afterward we strolled over to hear a Dixieland band at the little bandstand where Rehoboth Avenue meets the boardwalk. Then Mr. Jones and Meredith walked back to the cottage, and the three of us were on our own.

We wanted to do everything there was to do. We walked the length of the boardwalk, peered in all the shops, and decided to ride the Ferris wheel so we could look out over the ocean at the top. I liked that. First you're part of the noise and confusion down below, and then you're up there above it. Then you're down with the French fry smells, and then you're up with the salt air in your nostrils.

"Is it just my imagination, or are those guys watching us?" said Pamela.

"What guys?" I asked, looking down.

"The guys leaning against the fence," said Pamela.

"Don't let them know we're watching them," said Liz quickly. "What are they wearing?"

"How can I tell what they're wearing if I don't look at them?" Pamela said. "Wait'll we go down again and I'll check."

I got a glimpse of four guys, older than we were, by a fence at the back of the small amusement park there by the boardwalk. They were smiling our way and talking among themselves.

"When we get off, don't *linger*," Elizabeth said, and somehow that set us off. Pamela and I started laughing. That made the four guys smile even broader. One had a shaved head, another wore a blue bandana around his forehead. A third wore a cowboy hat, and the fourth had bleached hair. Early twenties, I decided.

The Ferris wheel was slowing down and we thought the guys would try to hit on us right away, but they stayed where they were by the fence. When Liz bent down to tie her sneaker, Pamela said, "You're *lingering!*"

We made it as far as the bumper cars, and Pamela said we absolutely could not leave until we'd ridden them. She got a car to herself, but I got in beside Liz, and then we saw the four guys getting into bumper cars too.

"They'll cream us!" said Liz, and when the cars started up with a jerk, she gripped the wheel firmly, her lips set, like we were on a military mission.

"We're not on a freeway, you know," I said. "Lighten up." She giggled nervously.

Whap! We were broadsided by the grinning guy in the blue bandana. I smelled the booze.

Wham! We got it from the rear by the guy with the shaved head. He grinned at us too, flashing the gold stud in his tongue.

Pamela, up ahead, seemed to be having a ball. Natural ability, maybe, but she wove deftly in and out of the cars, and it wasn't until the end that they got her cornered and she couldn't go anywhere.

All the cars stopped. This time I agreed with Liz not to linger. As Pamela stepped out of her car, the guy with the blue bandana reached out to grab her ankle, laughing, but she got away, and as soon as she reached us, we set out for the boardwalk double time and started home.

"Talk about *soused!*" Pamela said. "They reeked!"

"Hey!" came a voice from behind us. Then a whistle. "*Hey!* Wait up!"

"Keep walking," said Pamela.

"Hey!" came the voice, more insistent. "You with the long legs and the tight ass."

"The jerks!" said Liz, but secretly each of us wished it were her he was talking about. Since I have the shortest legs, I knew it wasn't me.

We left the boardwalk and went down a concrete ramp to the street below.

"How far from the house do you think we are?" Liz asked nervously.

"Five or six blocks over, I'd say," Pamela answered.

"Maybe we should have stayed on the boardwalk longer, where there are more lights," I said, eyeing the darkness ahead of us. But it was too late now.

"Hey, you with the thirty-four C tits," came a deeper voice. "Wait up! We got something for you."

"I'll bet," I murmured. "You think they'll follow us all the way back? Then they'll know where we're staying."

"Just hope we *make* it back," said Liz.

We had to stop for a car at the corner, and I glanced over my shoulder.

"There are five of them now," I said. "And one's the size of a refrigerator. I don't know where he came from."

"Speed up!" whispered Pamela. "Oh God, I show up with these guys, and Dad'll never take me anywhere again."

I began to look for places we could duck into to get away. It was about ten thirty, and some of the houses were dark back here away from the ocean.

Elizabeth's voice was shaky now: "Pamela, it's even darker on your block. I don't want to be with these guys back there."

"Where else can we go?" Pamela said. "We can't stop now."

The guys were only ten feet behind us. The house to our right was dark, but the one next to it was lit, and the front door was open. Balloons were tied to the handle of the screen, a celebration of some sort, and as the guys came up behind us, I whispered to Pam and Liz, "We're going in."

"*What?*" Liz whispered, but I nudged her to make the turn, and Pamela followed.

"Bye," I called to the guys behind us, and kept walking.

"Don't be in such a hurry!" said the guy with the shaved head, but we didn't stop.

I walked right up the steps, opened the screen, and said, "We're back!" And in we went.

An elderly woman sat in the middle of the couch, surrounded by tissue paper and ribbon, and three middle-aged women were gathering up paper cups and plates. A couple of men sat at the small table in the dining room and turned to stare at us.

I glanced out the screen. The five guys had stopped on the street and were looking up at the house.

"We had a wonderful time," I said, a little too loudly. The woman on the couch squinted at us.

"Alice, you should be in the movies," Liz whispered.

"You lost, young ladies?" one of the men said, getting up from the table and wiping crumbs off his shirt.

"We're really sorry to intrude," I apologized, lowering my voice, "but could you possibly pretend we live here for the next fifteen minutes or so?"

"Do we know you, sweetheart?" asked one of the women.

"No, but some guys are following us out there, and we don't want them to know where we're staying," said Pamela. "I'd call my dad to come get us, but it's a rental house and I don't know the number."

"Well, for goodness' sake!" said the woman on the couch. "You just help yourselves to some cake over there and that punch on the table, too. It's our fiftieth wedding anniversary, Bob's and mine."

"Congratulations!" Liz said.

The man with the crumbs walked over and shook our hands. "Bob Seifert," he said. "Pleased to meet you."

We each introduced ourselves.

The second man got up and peered out the door, then closed it. "Those the ones you're talking about?" he asked.

"Yes. If they think we live here, maybe they'll go away," Pamela said.

So we sat around drinking punch and eating cake and telling them all we'd done at the beach. Our little intrusion seemed exciting to them, and one of the women kept peeping out through the curtains, although we wished she wouldn't.

But a half hour later Liz reported that the guys were gone. So the two men escorted us back to our rental house and walked us right up to the door. We thanked them profusely.

"You girls be careful now," one of them said. "Can't ever be too careful at the beach."

By the time we got back to Silver Spring, I'd been gone four days—Friday through Monday—and I called the misses' sportswear department at Hecht's to see what time Juanita wanted me to come in on Tuesday, but she was on her dinner break. I left a message for her to call back.

Sylvia had bought some crabmeat, and I showed her how Meredith had made crab cakes. She loved my straw hat, and when Dad got home, I told them both about the trip. About volleyball on the sand and learning to duck under the waves. About Jerry and the cotton candy place and the guys in the bumper cars and how I'd got lost on my Jet Ski. Sylvia really laughed about that one.

"Oh, Alice, that could only happen to you!" she said. "I can just see you out there waving your shirt."

Dad laughed too. "Well, that little getaway made a nice end to summer, didn't it? I'm glad you got to go," he told me.

"I've still got two weeks left," I said. And then I remembered Lester. "Have you heard from Les?"

"Not a word," said Dad.

I frowned. "Shouldn't we check? Have you called his apartment?"

"I called once to invite him to dinner, but they said he was sleeping," Sylvia told me. "It's going to take time for him to get over Tracy. He just might not want to be sociable for a while."

I couldn't accept that. I couldn't believe there wasn't *something* I could do to cheer him up, but I was really too tired that evening to think of anything. Juanita still hadn't called by ten, so I decided to go in early the next day to play it safe.

At eight, I staggered out of bed, showered, and did my hair, then took a bus to Wheaton Plaza. I got to the store five minutes after it opened but figured I'd get points for coming in at ten, even though I didn't know what time they wanted me.

I took the escalator up to sportswear.

"Is Juanita here?" I asked the girl who was tagging a rack of fall pants.

"She went to the office for change. She'll be back in a minute," she said. I stuck my bag under the counter and folded some pants that were piled there.

"I'm Alice," I said to the girl.

"Hi. I'm Lonnie," she told me.

I could see Juanita's blue-black hair bobbing above the racks as she came back to sportswear. She was surprised to see me.

"I'm back!" I said. "We had a fabulous time!" When she didn't answer, I said, "I left a message yesterday for you to call me, and when you didn't, I figured I'd better come in at ten just in case."

Juanita looked at Lonnie, then at me. She came over and gently took me aside. "Alice, I'm afraid you don't work here anymore," she said.

I could only stare. "What?"

"You see, you didn't have permission to take four days off."

It still wasn't registering. "That was my only vacation, and it wasn't even a whole week!" I explained. "I *told* you when I was going and when I'd be back."

She tipped her head and gave me a slightly admonishing look. "Honey, you *told* me, you didn't ask. And I'm not the one who grants leave. I thought that surely you'd arranged it with the personnel office before you left, and that they'd send me someone to fill in. When you didn't punch your time card, Jennifer Martin came up to see if you were working. I told her you were on vacation, and she said it was the first she'd heard about it."

"But . . . but you're my supervisor!"

"I'm the supervisor of misses' sportswear, but I don't hire and fire. Jennifer was the one who hired you and the one you should have talked to about getting time off. And you know"—she touched my arm again—"nobody really has any vacation time coming until they've worked here a year."

I couldn't believe it. "No vacation?" I said weakly.

"Not when you're part-time, though they do give time off if we're not too busy."

Lonnie, of course, was listening to the whole conversation, putting a new shipment of shirts on hangers in slow motion.

Juanita went on: "You can go to the office and see if there's any chance of being rehired, but Jennifer was pretty upset. We were having that gigantic clearance sale, you remember, and this place was a zoo!"

I felt as small and low as a pin there on the floor.

"And, of course, now," Juanita went on, "we've hired Lonnie in your place. I'm sorry, Alice."

I took my bag out from under the counter. "I'm sorry too that I let you down," I said, my face warm with embarrassment. What a sheltered life I'd lived, really—working for my dad, taking time off for granted. Now I knew why he wanted me to get a taste of the outside world. How could I have thought I could just announce I was going to the ocean with friends and get an automatic okay?

"Bye, Juanita," I said.

She gave me a quick hug. "Live and learn, huh? Good luck, honey."

"Have a great time in Puerto Rico," I said.

I didn't go to the office. I didn't even go down to Burger King to see if Pamela still had a job. I went back to the bus stop and took the first one leaving the mall.

I'd been fired!

I couldn't wrap my mind around it. The first real outside job I'd ever had—an outside *paying* job—and I'd been sacked. I could feel the blood throbbing in my head and kept swallowing and swallowing as saliva gathered at the back of my throat.

I'd thought I was doing so well. I had reported

those shoplifters and got them arrested! How could they even think of letting me go without giving me another chance?

I didn't know if Sylvia would be home or not, but I couldn't bear to tell her how stupid I had been, so I didn't get off at my usual stop but stayed on till we got to the corner near the Melody Inn.

"Alice!" Marilyn said when she saw me. Lester's old girlfriend, now married, always greets me like a sister. "Well, for heaven's sake! Nice to see you!"

I managed a weak smile. "Is Dad around?" I asked.

"He's back in the office, I think," she said, and gave me a quizzical look.

I headed for the back of the store and almost collided with David, who was carrying a box of sheet music.

"Hey!" he said. "How's it going?"

"Hi," I said without answering, and went straight back to the office, closing the door behind me.

Dad was sorting through some papers on his desk and didn't even look up for a second. When he did, he blinked and looked again. "Al!" he said.

My chin wobbled, but I steeled myself. I promised myself I wouldn't cry. "I'm wondering . . . if we could go to lunch," I said.

"Lunch? It's only eleven o'clock. Didn't you eat any breakfast this morning?" he asked. And then, "I thought you'd be at work."

"So did I," I said, and waited a second longer to get up my courage. "Dad . . . I've been fired."

He sat back in his chair. "Fired?" he asked softly.

"Juanita told me when I went in. She said I ought to have cleared my time off with the office."

Dad looked at me with disbelief on his face. "You mean you didn't? You just went without telling them?"

"No, I told Juanita. I thought that was all I had to do. I thought *every*one got time off for a vacation."

Dad gave me a sorrowful smile. "The outside world doesn't work that way, does it?"

I hung my head. "I feel so stupid. So embarrassed. They were having a big clearance sale while I was gone, and I can just imagine what it was like with clothes piling up in the fitting rooms."

A tear escaped in spite of me. I imagined having to go the rest of my life telling all future employers that I'd left my employment at Hecht's because I'd been fired. "Now they've hired someone else," I sniffled. "Do you think I'll ever get another job?"

Dad smiled. "Oh, I think so. Everyone's entitled to a few youthful mistakes. Be honest. Tell your next employer what happened and how you'd never make that same mistake again." His smile grew even broader. "You'll make *others*, of course."

"That isn't exactly comforting," I said. "I'd thought I might want to work part-time at Hecht's all through the school year, and now I can't. I'm not even sure that I should. I don't know whether to try for a job somewhere else or not."

"I'm not sure it's a good idea, either, to try to hold down a part-time job during the school year, Al. Why don't you go out there and help David check in that order of sheet music? Make yourself useful, and we'll go get a sandwich later," Dad said. Then he grinned. "And if you need a good recommendation to a future employer, I'll give you one."

I smiled a little too. "Thanks, Dad," I said.

Songs with Aunt Sally

I always feel better after lunch with my dad. A
Philly cheesesteak sandwich with onions would
make almost anyone feel better. It didn't make my
unauthorized vacation any less stupid; it just gave
me some perspective. My life wasn't exactly ruined
because of it.

I walked all the way back home instead of taking the bus—penance, I guess. When I reached
our street, I noticed that the leaves on some of the
trees were already turning yellow and beginning
to curl. Fall was breathing down my neck. I called
Pamela's house to see if she was working. She
wasn't, and when she invited me over, I jumped
at the chance to get away. I put on shorts and
walked to her house.

"Well, don't feel too bad about it," she said
when I told her about my job. "I'm giving my
notice tomorrow because I don't think I should be

working during the school year. I've got to bring my grades up."

I don't think I'd been in her house five minutes before she got a call from her mom. We looked at the cell phone lying on Pamela's rug while she debated whether or not to answer.

"Sooner or later, Pamela . . . ," I told her.

She sighed and picked it up. "Want to listen?" she asked before she pressed SEND.

"Not particularly," I said, but she held it away from her ear anyway.

"Hi, honey. How you doing?" came her mother's chirpy voice.

"Doing okay, Mom. How about you?" said Pamela.

Her mother cut right to the chase. "Well, how did things go at the ocean?"

"It was fun," Pamela told her. "We had a great time. Did the beach, the rides, the Jet Ski. . . ." She looked at me and grinned. "Alice got lost on her Jet Ski, but we managed to get her back to shore."

I heard her mother laugh. "And Bill?" she asked. "What is this Meredith person like?"

"She's nice. Easy to get along with," said Pamela.

"Are they serious, do you think?"

Pamela took a deep breath and gave me a *Here goes* look. "I'd say so, Mom, seeing as how they're engaged."

"Oh . . . oh . . ." There was silence. A long silence. Pamela checked the phone to be sure there was still a connection. And finally we heard Mrs. Jones say, "I was afraid of this. Well . . . there's a chapter of my life that's closed, I guess. I wish I'd have lived it differently, but I didn't. And at some point"—her voice wavered, but she went on—"you have to pay the piper. But . . ."

Silences are really painful when you can only guess what's coming next. Pamela and I looked at each other uncertainly.

"But . . . the *next* chapter's unwritten, right? A blank slate?" she said.

"Whatever you want to make it, Mom," Pamela said.

After she hung up, Pamela and I studied each other without saying anything for a moment. "Sometimes . . . what you think is going to be the hardest isn't that bad at all," she said finally.

Pamela had been dreading that conversation with her mom, but maybe not as much as I was dreading telling Sylvia that I'd been fired. I'd stayed at Pamela's as long as I could, but it was time to get home and help Sylvia make dinner. We didn't have school this week, but teachers had to be there.

When I walked inside, Sylvia was reading a

magazine, her feet propped on the arm of the sofa. "Oh, good! I didn't know if you'd be home for dinner or not," she said when she saw me. "Ben will be late, so it's just us girls. What do—?"

"Sylvia," I said quickly, "I got fired."

Her eyebrows questioned me. "What?"

"I didn't get permission from the right person to take that long weekend at the beach, and they let me go."

"Really?" She swung her legs around and sat upright.

I flopped down beside her. "How could I have been so stupid?"

"Inexperienced, maybe, but not stupid," she said gently.

"No, I've been incredibly spoiled, working for Dad all this time."

"Well, maybe so." She smiled and gave me a hug. "Let's just say that Ben was right and you needed a little more contact with the real world. Any chance they'll reconsider?"

"Juanita didn't think so. They were having this colossal sale, and I wasn't there for it. I don't know if I would have wanted to work during the school year or not, but I can't bear the thought of this on my record. I was thinking of writing a letter of apology to the woman who hired me. Do you think that's a good idea?"

"I think it's a *very* good idea. And be sure to tell her all you learned while you were working there. Employers like to hear that."

We sat quietly for a moment or two. "This is the way life is, right? Great times followed by something lousy. Sad, even." I thought of Molly.

"Sort of," she said, and smiled a little. "It's a roller coaster, not a merry-go-round. But sometimes there are lots of good things one right after another and a sad thing only once in a while."

"And some people have lots of sad things and a good thing only once in a while."

"That's true," she said. "Life isn't fair."

"Does it ever bother you? I mean, do you find yourself worrying what the next bad thing will be?"

"I look at it this way," she said. "If we're going to ruin what good times we have by worrying they won't last, then we might as well not have good times at all, because what difference does it make if we're going to be miserable anyway?"

I hadn't thought about it that way.

"Enjoy what you can, Alice," she said. "And when life hits you in the stomach, deal with it then. Don't try to figure everything out in advance."

I got up. "Okay. I'm going to write that letter," I said. I started upstairs, then stopped. "Any word yet from Lester?"

"Only that he can't come to dinner tomorrow. He's finishing a paper for his course."

I sat down at my desk and began the letter to Jennifer Martin. I read it over twice to make sure I'd said everything I wanted to say. Then I sealed and stamped it. But the fact was, I was getting distracted by thoughts of Lester. I hadn't known him to refuse a dinner invitation very often. Was that even true that he was working on a paper? Weren't summer school courses over before the end of August, even in graduate school? He was holed up in his apartment, sad, lonely, dejected, depressed, and if nobody else was going to do something about it, I would. Lester's twenty-fourth birthday was coming up, and I was determined he wouldn't spend it alone.

Aunt Sally called that evening "just to talk," and I sure wasn't going to tell her about getting fired. I didn't want still another person disappointed in me.

"School's about to start up soon," she said. "How has your summer been, dear?"

"It's gone by pretty quick," I told her. "I'm getting eager to go back, actually. I miss being on the newspaper staff."

"Oh, I can imagine! Sixteen is an exciting year," she said. "My grandma used to say it was our most dangerous year—Marie's and mine."

Anytime she mentioned my mother, I was interested. "Dangerous? Why?"

"She said that's the year we'd be introduced to
the most temptations."

"Who introduced you?" I asked. All I could
think was that *my* sixteenth year must be passing
me by, because I hadn't been introduced to any
temptations that were particularly appealing.

"Grandma meant that we would be offered alcohol and cigarettes and other such things. In fact,
when she took care of us sometimes when we
were smaller, she used to sing songs out of her old
school songbook to prepare us. She even made
Marie and me memorize some of them."

"Songs?"

"To sing if we were tempted."

Les always said that Mom loved to sing, but I
thought she loved songs from *Showboat*. "What
kind of songs?" I asked.

"Oh, she had one for every occasion, let me tell
you. I remember the day she tried to teach us to
make piecrusts. Marie was ten—I was fourteen—
and the last thing on our minds was pie crust.
Ours came out all sticky and doughy, and Marie
and I just gave up. Grandma marched us straight
to the piano and made us learn 'Never Say Fail.'"
And Aunt Sally began to sing it over the telephone:

Keep working, 'tis wiser than sitting aside,
And dreaming and sighing, and waiting the tide;
In life's earnest battle those only prevail
Who daily march onward, and never say fail.

I tried hard not to laugh. "Did it work?" I asked.

"No, Grandma had to make the pies herself. But, oh, she was a stickler for learning those songs. Alcohol? She wouldn't let it near the house. She wouldn't even keep vanilla in the cupboard for fear we'd drink it."

"You're kidding!" I said.

"I was only eleven when I had to memorize 'Touch Not the Cup.' Do you want to hear it? Marie had to learn it later."

I wanted to, if only to connect with my mother.

Touch not the cup, it is death to the soul;
Touch not the cup, touch not the cup;
Many I know who have quaffed from that bowl;
Touch not the cup, touch it not.
Little they tho't that the demon was there,
Blindly they drank and were caught in its snare;
Then of that death-dealing bowl, oh, beware;
Touch not the cup, touch it not.

"Wow!" I said. "And I can't even sing!"

"There were four verses, and we had to learn

them all," said Aunt Sally. "Marie learned them faster than I did, because the sooner she did, the sooner she could go out to play. I believe our grandmother had a song for whatever she wanted to teach us. Even Grandpa got in the act now and then, if only to make her stop." Aunt Sally laughed. "His favorite was titled 'Don't Talk If You've Nothing to Say.'" That cracked us up. "I miss them, the old folks," Aunt Sally said. "But someday I suppose you'll be laughing at me, too."

"Aunt Sally, some of my most interesting conversations have been with you," I said. "How's Uncle Milt?"

"Well, we manage to keep busy, Alice. Your uncle's taking more medications than he used to, but there's certainly never a day we don't have enough to do."

"And Carol?" I asked.

"She's dating a nice man now, so we'll see what comes of that. Is everyone all right in your family?"

"Yes," I told her, omitting the part about Lester.

"Life goes by in a rush," said Aunt Sally. "Let us hear from you now and then."

"You will," I said.

At dinner the following night I asked, "Could we have a surprise party for Lester for his birthday? It's only ten days away."

"I think we could manage that. A party, anyway. I'm not sure about the surprise part," said Dad. "What were you thinking?"

"Oh . . . I thought we could invite his room-mates and some of his friends. I'll take care of the invitations if you'll furnish the food. But we'd need to make sure he comes over."

We thought about that a minute. "He's good at taking us to the airport when we need him," said Sylvia. "We could ask him to come by that night and pick us up—tell him that we're leaving town for a few days."

Dad checked his calendar. "His birthday's on a Sunday this year. Why don't we have him over for dinner that night to celebrate, but hold the real party on the following Friday. We'll have to check with his housemates to see if he's free."

"Let's do it!" said Sylvia. "That will be fun!"

I went up to my room and started a guest list. Lester's two housemates—Paul Sorenson and George Palamas. They'd have to come separately and stay for only half the evening each, of course, because one of them always has to be there for old Mr. Watts. I'd invite his old girlfriend Marilyn, just because she worked for Dad, my three best friends, Pamela, Liz, and Gwen . . .

But then I got carried away. Why not Rosalind's brother Billy, who used to play in Lester's band, the Naked Nomads, back in Takoma Park? Of course, then I'd need to invite Rosalind. What about Lester's baseball buddies? Friends he knew at the university? His roommates should be able to help me with my list.

Dad called Les and confirmed that he could drive them to the airport Friday evening, September ninth.

"Did he sound okay?" I asked.

"He sounded like Lester, Al. Sometimes he's up, sometimes he's down. I don't expect him to be playing a harmonica and tap-dancing, okay?"

I got all the phone numbers I could and started calling, leaving messages when no one was home. Parties can get pretty complicated. They sound simple when you first start thinking about them. Then you have to be sure you have enough chairs, and what about plates? Cold food or hot? Soft drinks or coffee? Should we have beer? Should there be music? Dancing? Inside or out? And what about decorations?

I was tired already and couldn't expect Dad and Sylvia to take my idea and run with it. Dad was gearing up for the big Labor Day sale at work, and Sylvia was making lesson plans for the first week of school. I asked my friends to help me.

"I think the best decorations would be photographs of Lester from birth till now. That's what *we* do for birthday parties," said Gwen, and added, "Funerals, too."

"Now, that makes me feel *real* good!" I said.

"*I* think we should get some *Muscle & Fitness* magazines, cut out pictures of bodybuilders, remove their heads, and put Lester's face there instead," said Pamela. "We could put them all over the house."

We loved that idea, too.

"I'll get the magazines," said Pamela.

"I'll buy some poster board," said Gwen.

"I'll look through our old photos and see what I can find," I promised, and Liz said she'd bring some streamers.

"Don't expect this bash to work miracles on Les," Gwen warned me.

"Okay. I won't expect miracles. Instead, I'll expect the worst," I said, sinking into a chair. "I'm going to expect that not only will everyone we've invited show up, but that they'll bring their children and parents and boyfriends as well. I'm going to expect that at least one person will get sick at the party, somebody else will get drunk, somebody will get offended at something, and it will probably rain. Then, if some of those things *don't* happen, I'll be happy."

"Is that going to be your life's philosophy?"

asked Gwen. "Expect the worst, and it will usually be better than what you thought?"

I thought about what Sylvia had said. "No," I said. "I'm going to enjoy the good things that happen and deal with the bad as they come along. How's that?"

"You're getting there," said Gwen.

"You'll never guess who came into the store today," Dad said when he got home from work. "Loretta Jenkins. Loretta Jenkins James, to be exact."

"Oh my God!" I said. "She's still married?"

"Very much so," said Dad, "and her little girl is going on three years old already."

If there was ever someone I would have voted most likely not to succeed, it was Loretta Jenkins. She used to run the Gift Shoppe there at the Melody Inn. Loretta was a cheerful, laid-back person with a huge mane of curly hair, which she wore like a sunburst around her head.

While she was working for Dad, she got pregnant. She was engaged and then married in no time. She had morning sickness like you wouldn't believe. The last time I'd seen Loretta, in fact, she was bending over the toilet at the Melody Inn. She and her new husband didn't have enough money to get their own place, so they were moving in with his parents. I thought they'd be lucky if the marriage lasted a year.

"Not only are they still married," Dad said, "but she told me they have an apartment now, her husband has a better job, and she's taking a couple of night school courses. Happy as a clam."

Hooray for her! I thought. It just goes to show that sometimes a couple with almost nothing going for them can make it if they really want to. And then I had an idea.

"Do you have her phone number?" I asked. "I want to call and invite her to Lester's party. Wouldn't that be a hoot?"

"It would be a surprise, all right," Dad said.

16

Junior Year

We tried to squeeze all we could out of the end of summer. Pamela gave her notice at Burger King. The day camp where Liz had been working had ended two weeks ago, and Gwen had finished her internship at the National Institutes of Health. I was feeling sort of unsettled. I'd promised myself that I'd visit Molly at least once a week. I'd *thought* of it, but I hadn't called since we got back from the ocean. But she had a big family—four sisters, two of them coming clear across the country to be with her. Did she really need me?

You can think of all kinds of reasons not to do something that makes you uncomfortable. And visiting Molly was uncomfortable sometimes, because I didn't always know what to say that would make her feel better. And then I remembered what Pamela said, about friends being family. I went to the phone and called Molly.

* * *

Over the last week before school we worked on the decorations for Lester's party and bought some clothes for the new semester. Then on Saturday we went to each other's houses to redecorate our bulletin boards. It was like those TV shows where people redecorate each other's houses. We made each person leave her bedroom, and she couldn't come back till we'd finished. Gwen's house was first. She sat on the floor out in the hall while we took over. "Don't take down that picture of my grandmother," she called to us. "If she comes in here and discovers she's not the center of my universe anymore, I'll hear about it for the next six months."

We put her grandma's picture back on the board, in the very center, inside a big red cutout heart that Liz made. Pamela and I had pictures of Gwen, though, that we'd taken at Camp Overlook last summer when we were all assistant counselors, so we had come armed and ready.

I carefully cut out a figure of Gwen jumping into the lake, arms wrapped around her knees in a cannonball jump. I tilted her around so she appeared to be lying on her back. Then I glued her onto a picture of one of the counselors at camp, his arms holding out a giant-size pizza. It looked like Gwen, not the pizza, was in his arms.

"Perfect!" Liz squealed.

"Okay, you guys, what are you up to in there?" came Gwen's voice from out in the hall. "Don't put up anything my mom shouldn't see."

Pamela had a picture of Gwen leaning down to talk to Latisha, our problem camper. We cut out Gwen from the photo and pasted it to a picture of another guy at camp, looking up from his lunch, so it appeared that the two were kissing.

"Bingo!" said Pamela.

Then there was the picture of Gwen in New York on the ferry, with the Statue of Liberty in the background. She had one hand on her chest, holding on to the strap of her shoulder bag. We put a torch in that hand and a crown on her head, and presto! Another version of the statue.

"Oh, Gwen, you'll be famous!" I said. "People will come from all over the world to see you!"

"You're not taking off my clothes, are you?" she warned from around the corner.

Of course we put back some of her own mementos: a dried-up corsage from a dance; an autograph from her favorite author; her membership card in the National Honor Society; a picture of her church choir; a ticket stub from a rock concert. . . .

"Okay!" Pamela said at last. We made Gwen close her eyes, then led her back inside the bedroom and stood her in front of her bulletin board.

JUNIOR YEAR • 225

"Open!" I told her.

Gwen yelped when she saw the picture of herself in her bathing suit pinned at the top of the board. We had glued the rounded halves of pencil erasers on her breasts and padded her hips with part of a bunion pad, giving her an hourglass figure. On the side of the picture, with arrows pointing to the appropriate places, we had written, *Gwen Wheeler, Miss America, bust 38, waist 24, hips 38.*

Her folks heard all the laughing and came in to see it too. Gwen's mom, a lawyer at the Justice Department, wears jeans and a T-shirt at home on weekends. She's short and shapely like her daughter, with dimples in both cheeks. Mr. Wheeler is as tall as his wife is short, and I think he works with computers.

"So *that's* what went on at that camp last summer," her dad said, chuckling, pointing to a picture of Gwen in her bunk bed, the covers pulled up to her chin. Only we'd pasted the head of one of the guys on the pillow next to her, and Gwen really screamed when she saw that.

"Don't I wish!" she said.

"Show these to your brothers when they come home," said her mom. "They'll get a kick out of them."

Then it was on to my house, where they took

the photos of me in awkward positions at camp, cut me out of the pictures, and pinned me up on my bulletin board with names of silly exercises on them: The Side-Straddle Hop; The Squat-Grunt-Stretch; The Torso Twist; and The Butt Tightener.

At Liz's, while she played with her little brother in the next room, we pinned up close-ups of her face. We had carefully drawn different makeup schemes on each one and changed her hair as well: a Dolly Parton wig in one, a Cher wig in another, her eyebrows pencil-thin in a third, a beauty mark on her cheek. We even glued false eyelashes on it to make it more real.

We'd saved Pamela's house till last, not because our decorating was so explosive, but because her dad might be. According to Pamela, no "person of color" had ever crossed their threshold. No Latino, no Asian, not even a person whose last name ended in an *i* or an *a*. Had he remembered our mentioning Gwen when we were at the beach?

"So what's the worst that can happen?" Gwen asked as we went up the steps.

"That he won't let either one of us in the house and I'll have to spend the night at your place," Pamela told her.

"Not to worry," said Gwen.

We went in and could hear Mr. Jones puttering around in the kitchen.

"I've got some friends with me, Dad," Pamela called. "We're going to fix up my room a little."

"Okay," he said, and came to the kitchen doorway holding a skillet and dishtowel. He stopped and stared stonily at Gwen.

"Oh, this is Gwen Wheeler, the one I told you about," Pamela added brightly. "The *brain*. We were counselors together at camp last summer."

Gwen smiled at Pamela's dad. "Hello," she said.

Mr. Jones gave an almost imperceptible nod, turned, and went back inside the kitchen.

Pamela gave us a quick *Well, we got that far* look and led us upstairs.

We'd planned Pamela's bulletin board far in advance and had gathered pictures of people in different professions. We cut out Pamela's head from photos at camp and our New York trip and pasted them on assorted pictures of people in uniform: a scuba-diving suit; a firefighter's suit; a nurse's uniform; an acrobat. There was Pamela as a ballet dancer, an astronaut, a doorman, a maid, a soldier, and, of course, Pamela as a stripper with nothing but pasties on her breasts.

Up at the top of the bulletin board we tacked cutout letters that read: THE PAMELA POSSIBILITIES. Then we let her in to see it.

"Oh, I *love* it!" she cried. "Omigod, look at *that* one!"

We outdid ourselves, it's true.

Mr. Jones came upstairs to get a pair of shoes, and Pamela dragged him in to see her bulletin board. He came unsmiling, reluctant. But when he saw the pictures, he had to smile a little.

"You end up any of those, Pamela, except *that* one," he said, pointing to the stripper, "and it'll be okay with me." We laughed.

As he started to leave the room, he turned to Gwen and said, "What'd you say your last name was?"

"Wheeler," she told him.

"I think the guy who fixes my car is a Wheeler," Mr. Jones said. "Your dad a car mechanic?"

"No. He designs computer software," Gwen said.

"Oh . . . well, there're a lot of Wheelers around, I guess," said Pamela's dad.

"Yeah," said Pamela. "Same as Joneses." After he left, she thrust one fist triumphantly in the air.

When we got outside, we were feeling so proud of ourselves that we didn't want the day to end.

"On to Molly's!" I said. "If she doesn't have a bulletin board, we'll make one!"

And so we did.

Sunday was Lester's birthday, and Sylvia had invited him over for dinner as planned. I was afraid he wouldn't come, but we were making all his favorite dishes. That lured him, I guess: filet mignon, baked potatoes with sour cream, green beans with almonds, Caesar salad. I made his favorite for dessert, too, a German chocolate cake—and it turned out fantastic!

I saw the look of pleasure on his face when he tasted it. "*You* made this, Al? It's great!" he said.

I beamed. Mostly I was happy that Les had an appetite. At the same time, though, he seemed distracted, depressed. I guess he wouldn't be normal if he wasn't.

"How's the new semester going at the U?" I asked him.

"Hasn't started yet," he answered.

"You said you plan to finish up this next year, Les?" Sylvia said. "How's the thesis coming?"

"Slowly," he told her. "I've hit a couple of snags, but my adviser thinks we can work it out."

I remembered the title he'd told me: "In Defense of Partiality and Friendship: A Critique of Utilitarianism and Kantianism." I was sure I'd never be able to understand it. I couldn't even understand the title.

More silence as coffee cups were raised and lowered.

"Marilyn said to tell you happy birthday," Dad told him.

"Yeah. Well . . . ," Les said. Then, "What time

did you want me to pick you up on Friday?"

"No sooner than seven. The flight doesn't leave till ten o'clock."

"And you said you're going to London?" Les asked.

"Isn't it crazy?" said Sylvia. "It's only for a few days, but a customer is giving us tickets to a concert—the London Philharmonic Orchestra— and a Shakespeare play at the renovated Globe Theatre. He got a package deal for him and his wife, but she's sick, so they gave it to us. It was so generous of him!"

How could Sylvia sit there and lie with a straight face? I wondered. Her story sounded so authentic, it was scary.

"We'd invite you to come for dinner first, but I'm afraid things will be pretty hectic here," she continued. I knew she'd said that so he wouldn't come early and see people arriving at the party.

"That's okay. I haven't been too hungry lately," Les said. He looked at me. "Don't tell me Alice is going to be here by herself."

"I'll be staying at Elizabeth's," I said. "Not that I *couldn't*. I know how to run a house, Lester. I can lock the doors and water the plants and sort the mail like anyone else."

Lester didn't stay much longer. He opened our gifts—a check from Dad, a shirt from Sylvia, a CD from me, and candy from Aunt Sally and Uncle Milt—and then he went out to his car. "See you Friday," he called.

"We are such good liars!" I said to Sylvia as we watched him drive away.

"Sinfully so," she said. "But he needs some cheering up, you can tell."

"He did clean his plate, however," said Dad. "That counts for something."

On Labor Day we had our last swim at Mark's. Pamela, Liz, and I wore straw hats we'd bought at the beach and looked like something out of a nineteenth-century paintings—from the neck up, anyway. The other girls had to try them on, and even some of the guys wore them for a while. The Stedmeisters had a barbecue for us. Mark's dad, short and dumpy, stood at the grill cooking hamburgers to order, and Mark's mom put out potato salad and chips and veggies and dips.

"You've been so nice to put up with us all these years," I said to Mrs. Stedmeister as she brought out some brownies.

She seemed almost teary at the compliment, as though she had been waiting all this time for somebody to say that. I was ashamed I hadn't thanked them before.

"We like seeing Mark's friends," she said. "It's

been a pleasure to have you." I guess if you're an only child, like Mark, you want a lot of friends around.

If she noticed Jill and Karen smoking, she didn't say anything. As long as it wasn't marijuana, I suppose she'd figure she'd let it go.

"When did you start smoking?" I asked Jill later.

"Couple months, and I've lost four pounds," Jill said. "It's the way French women keep their figures, you know."

"Curbs the appetite," said Karen.

"And your lungs?" asked Gwen.

"We'll worry about our lungs when we're sixty-five," said Jill, inhaling and blowing the smoke above her head.

"I worry about my skin," I said. "Sylvia says that smoking's the fastest way to look like a wrinkled prune. That and sunbathing. Dries out the skin."

Jill shrugged, but Karen, I noticed, took only a couple more drags of her cigarette, then stamped it out and frowned at no one in particular.

Keeno came by without Brian, and Patrick and Justin were there. Yolanda brought a boyfriend. We always manage to have a crowd.

"How did the landscaping job go this summer?" I asked Patrick as we sat with our legs in the pool, paper plates on our laps, as he devoured a second burger.

"Good for my arms and legs and wallet," he said, and he really did look huskier. "Takes me forever to tan, though."

"The trials of the redhead," I told him.

"Yeah. Send me a sympathy card." He grinned. Then, "Hey, we might have a class together this semester."

"Really?"

"I put off World History last year to squeeze in an economics course. Have you picked up your schedule yet? I got mine this week, and World History's second period."

"I'll check," I said. "That would be great."

"Yeah, I could steal your homework," he said.

"I can't imagine you *ever* needing something from me," I told him.

Patrick had to leave early, but the conversation turned to school, and we started to get nostalgic. September had arrived, the Stedmeisters would be closing their pool, and the summer of our sixteenth year would soon be only a memory. "We ought to take a picture," someone said. "Anybody have a camera?"

No one did, so Mark went inside the house and brought out his dad's digital. I was sorry Patrick left early, and, just for the sake of a picture, I was sorry Brian was missing too. I hated the thought that we might be slowly breaking apart, going in different directions—that we had to take whatever time we could get with the old crowd and not worry too much about what we'd all be doing next year.

"Hold it!" said Keeno. "We don't want an ordinary picture. I think we ought to have a mystery person in it." He looked us over. "I think we ought to dress Alice up as a guy."

"Yeah," said Justin, grinning. "That bikini top has got to go."

"Ha-ha," I said.

"Seriously," said Keeno. "Mark, get some clothes and a cap, and let's turn her into a boy. Three years from now we'll look at the picture and say, 'Who was that?'"

"And turn you into a babe?" I said.

"Yeah! Let's give Keeno a makeover!" said Liz.

So everyone set to work. Pamela pinned my hair up, and they put a baseball cap on my head. I pulled on a pair of Mark's jeans and loafers and a camouflage vest. Jill took eyeliner pencil and gave me a mustache and sideburns, darkened my eyebrows.

"Hey! You look studly!" said Pamela.

But we had the most fun with Keeno. Jill went in the bathroom and exchanged her 34D bra for a T-shirt, and we put the bra on Keeno with an orange in each cup. He pretended to fall forward with the weight of it. Penny put her flowered top over the bra but left it unbuttoned in front so we could see the bra, and Jill made a sarong out of her cover-up and tied that around Keeno's waist. We put Liz's butterfly thongs on his feet, and his heels hung over the backs.

"Oh, man, Keeno, you are *hot*!" I laughed. He blew me a kiss.

"What do we do about his hair?" said Karen. "Turban?"

When Mark went into the house again, his mom got in the act and brought out a box of layered cotton. She showed us how to comb it into platinum blond curls. We put a bandana around Keeno's head and tucked the curls in around the edge. The guys all whistled.

Then we posed—Keeno and me in the center, with my arm around his shoulder and Keeno standing flirtatiously, one hand on his hip. Mark's dad came out and took several shots of the group, and then Keeno and I spent the rest of the evening playing our appropriate roles. Funny what it does to you. I found myself sitting with one ankle propped on my other knee. Keeno really played the feminine role too, crossing his legs at the ankles.

When Mr. Stedmeister printed the photos out and brought copies to us, it really did look as though a new couple had joined the group.

"You're so *cute* together!" Jill said.

"You'd make a good couple," said Penny.

Keeno and me? Oh, I don't think so.

As it turned out, Patrick and I did have that class together. We're allowed to come in before school starts to pick up our schedules. So with school beginning on Wednesday, Dad drove Pam and Liz and me over to the high school the day before, and we got in line outside the office. We all like to get the room assignments in advance—put stuff in our lockers. Decorate them, even. It was fun seeing kids we hadn't talked to since June— catch up on what everyone was doing.

Lori and Leslie were standing just in front of us. They were still a couple and excitedly told us about their summer internship for the National Park Service.

"What were you doing?" I asked.

"Clearing sections of the Appalachian Trail," Lori explained. "We worked with a team—slept in tents, and in the evenings we had seminars on wildlife, rocks, trees . . . all sorts of things."

"Next year we'll work on another section of trail," said Leslie. "It'll look great on our résumés when we apply for career status."

Patrick was in line too. He'd picked up his schedule last Friday, and now he was back trying to replace his lunch hour with calculus.

"Patrick, when will you *eat*?" I asked.

"Don't worry," he said. "I eat on the way to class. I don't suffer, believe me."

Everyone else seemed so focused. Gwen had taken exams for two advanced placement courses, and I was simply sailing along, happy to be average. Was that so awful? I asked myself. Did everyone have to be in the top 10 percent?

"Now, this is the closest stairway to the gym. . . . ," we heard a voice saying, and I turned to see one of the guidance counselors doing freshman orientation, a group of wide-eyed ninth graders following close at her heels. One anxious-looking boy was even taking notes. *Just two years ago that was us,* I thought, excited and scared, regarding upperclassmen as gods, never imagining we could ever be that self-assured. "If you get confused," the counselor went on, "all you have to do is ask directions."

We grinned at each other, remembering the many times upperclassmen had sent us in exactly the opposite direction.

"And if you're late to class," the counselor said, "it's not the end of the world. I think you'll find our teachers here are freshman-friendly. But remember: The counseling offices are the most freshman-friendly spots in the whole school. Come by with any problem at all, at school or at home. Come by to tell us how things are going. To share good news. Come by just to say hello! We're always glad to see you. If my door's open, just walk in. If it's not, pick up the green folder outside my door and pencil in your name in one of the time slots. . . ."

My line moved forward, but I stood rooted to the floor. I thought of Mrs. Plotkin, my sixth-grade teacher, my favorite teacher in the whole wide world. I thought of Sylvia Summers and the day I'd cried in her seventh-grade English class when I recited the wrong poem, a poem that reminded me of my mother. The way Sylvia had put me at ease. And I knew at that moment that what I'd been thinking about off and on for the last couple of years was what I really wanted to do: I wanted to work in a school. I wanted to be that high school guidance counselor with the reassuring smile. I wanted my office to be the most welcoming place. I wanted to be there for all the Alices that would come along. For bright kids like Gwen and Patrick. For slow kids like Amy. For kids facing tough decisions. Sick kids and kids with mixed-up parents.

I decided that after the new semester began, I would put my name on the sign-up sheet outside the counselor's office. I'd sit down with Mrs. Bailey and ask about the courses I should be taking now. About the colleges with the best guidance programs. Things I should know or think about to be a counselor.

Someone nudged me from behind, and I caught up with the line outside the school office. Then I watched Mrs. Bailey direct her small band of freshmen to the school cafeteria for refreshments, then head down to the gym to gather up her next little group.

Everything seems fresh and new when you go back to school in September. The next morning I noticed that the hallways had been repainted, the floors waxed, the faucets and water fountains repaired, the windows washed. . . .

I wished I could have driven to school—we hated the bus—but even if I had my own car, Dad says I can't have any passengers other than family until the end of December. I am *sooooo* looking forward to that. Liz won't be sixteen for a couple of months yet, and Pamela and Gwen don't have cars either, so we're stuck with the bus for a while.

There was a meeting of the newspaper staff right after school the first day. We always rush to get out that first issue because it has to list new rules and procedures, introduce new teachers. We need to let students know about changes in the cafeteria, the dress code—stuff that isn't particularly fun to write about. Fortunately, the news editor has to do most of that. As a roving reporter, I get to do more of the fun stuff.

I was wondering what I'd say to Sam Mayer, one of our photographers. I hadn't seen him around all summer. What do you ever say to an ex-boyfriend when you were the one who did the breaking up? But Miss Ames said he was already on assignment getting a photo of all the new teachers.

We still met in Room 17, but the editor in chief had changed. He was a tall, thin guy named Scott Lynch, and another senior, Jacki Severn, was the new features editor. She came to our first meeting with a page full of ideas for feature stories, which was good in a way, except that they took up her whole page, I noticed. She hadn't left any room for *our* ideas.

"I've got a great idea for the first issue," she said. "I just found out that one of our seniors, Molly Brennan, has leukemia and may not be coming back to school for a while. I want to do a story on her, but I'll have to interview her immediately to make the first issue."

"Molly?" said Miss Ames. "Oh, I'm so sorry to hear that!"

I stared. "How did you find out?" I asked Jacki.

"Oh, we editors have our ways," she said coyly. "Of course, I'll have to be very diplomatic about it."

"But does Molly *want* you to do a story on her? Isn't that sort of private?" I asked. "She may not want you to advertise it especially."

"I didn't say advertise, I said write," said Jacki. "We're both seniors. So it would be like one senior confiding in another. A sort of sister-to-sister chat."

Scott cut in. "Molly's got to want to do this, Jacki."

"Yes, Jacki. Make sure you're not imposing," said Miss Ames.

"I don't see what you're all so upset about!" Jacki said. "There's nothing shameful about having cancer."

"I didn't say it was shameful," I said. "I said it was private, and there's a difference."

"Leave it to me," Jacki said. "I'll just go for a friendly visit and take notes, but if in the end she doesn't want me to publish the story, we won't. Don, would you be available tomorrow afternoon to take pictures if it's a go?"

The senior photographer didn't look any happier about it than I did. "Only if Molly is willing," he said.

Jacki made some notes to herself and looked annoyed with the rest of us. I was annoyed too when the meeting was over, and it didn't help my mood any that Tony Osler, sports editor for another year, leered at me and said, "Hey, sexy! Three times a week, huh?"

Brian had obviously widely circulated those sex quiz answers, and I knew I'd probably have to deal with this a few more times before it became yesterday's news. So I just said, "Are those things still floating around? Which version did you get? I sent him about five."

Tony looked confused.

"It was the only way to get him to stop," I said, stuffing my books in my backpack and walking out.

I called Molly as soon as I got home. "Listen, Jacki Severn is features editor this year, and she found out you're sick. She's going to call you and try to set up an interview for tomorrow—photographer and everything," I told her.

"You've got to be kidding," Molly said.

"I wish I were. I wanted to warn you."

"What does she want? A picture of me lying in bed with a rose on my chest?" Molly asked.

"I don't know. Something like that, I suppose. A sisterly chat, is the way she described it to the staff."

"The nerve!" said Molly. "Sure, she can come and take pictures if I can go over the next time she has the flu and take pictures of her puking in the toilet."

"You go, girl!" I said.

"No, wait a minute," said Molly. "I've got a better idea. . . ."

On Thursday after school we heard the doorbell ring as Jacki arrived at the Brennan house, photographer at her side. Molly's mom answered and told them to go upstairs, that Molly was in bed.

"We won't wake her, will we?" I could hear Jacki asking.

"I don't think so," said her mom.

Jacki entered Molly's bedroom, Don, the photographer, trailing reluctantly behind, and found Molly on the bed, surrounded by Pamela and Gwen and Liz and me, all sharing a pizza in our sweats and flannel pajama bottoms.

We had accented Molly's big blue eyes with mascara and eyeliner, put blush on her cheeks and gloss on her lips. She was wearing the black cap with the red sequins.

"Oh!" Jacki said. "I didn't know you had company. I can come back."

"No, it's fine!" said Molly. "Now or not at all. I only allow photographers on Thursdays."

We tried not to laugh.

Jacki just had to know this was a put-on, but it didn't stop her. She conducted the interview with all of us offering chirpy comments. Molly really mugged for the camera, striking one movie-star pose after another, and finally Jacki said bravely, "Well, I think we've done all we can here. Thanks so much, Molly, for letting us come by, and the whole *Edge* staff sends you our best wishes for a speedy recovery."

"I don't know about speedy, but I'll do the best I can," Molly said.

After Jacki and the photographer left, we rolled off the bed laughing.

"That's one interview that won't make the paper, I'll bet," I said. "I don't think that's quite the story she had in mind."

17

Party

I was getting nervous. A few people had called to say they couldn't make it to Les's party, but some hadn't replied to my phone messages at all. I'd been able to locate only one of the guys Les played baseball with, and he said he'd tell the others, and I'd left it to George Palamas to invite some of Lester's friends from the U. We had no idea how many to expect.

On Friday, Gwen and Liz and Pamela came over right after school, and we were glad the party was planned for that day, because rain was forecast for the next. It was warm, but a gentle breeze was blowing, fluttering the blue-checked tablecloth on the long metal fold-out table in the backyard that would hold the food.

Sylvia had ordered huge trays of gourmet sandwiches from a deli, and we furnished the rest— macaroni salad, tomatoes and mozzarella, platters of fruit and veggies, and a couple of chocolate fudge cakes.

I went up in my room for a final check in the mirror. I'll have to say I looked hot. I was wearing tight white pants and a black halter top, exposing most of my back. Black strappy sandals with short heels. Too bad we hadn't invited any guys my age; Lester's friends would have to do.

As I started to turn away, I saw my mother's eyes watching me. There's a photo on my dresser of me on my mom's lap. She was wearing a blue dress with white buttons, and I was playing with those buttons and laughing. I was probably about two.

Oh, Mom, I thought. *Look at me now.* Dad told me once that of all his daughters-in-law, Gramps had said he liked Marie best because of her smile. I bent over and kissed the picture before I went downstairs.

The streamers were strung on the back porch, the beer on ice, folding chairs around the lawn, and a CD player at the ready. We'd start our guests on the veggies and cheese, we decided, but wouldn't bring out the rest of the food till everyone was there.

We'd told guests to come at six thirty sharp, and we were putting the finishing touches on everything when the doorbell rang at six.

"I'm not even dressed yet!" Sylvia said, starting for the stairs.

"I'll get it," I said, and opened the front door.

There stood a woman in her early twenties in jeans and a T-shirt, with a wild mane of frizzy hair around her head.

"Loretta!" I said.

"Alice!" We threw ourselves in each other's arms. Here she was, a half hour early and looking great. Her hair was still bushy but was well-trimmed, and she was slimmer than she'd been back in her days at the Melody Inn.

She smiled broadly, and I remembered how she used to smile that way at Lester.

"So how are you?" I asked, after introducing her to my friends.

"I'm great!" she said. "My little girl is amazing, my husband's got a job he likes, we finally got our own apartment, and I'm hoping to have another baby. How's that for a progress report?"

Dad introduced her to Sylvia, and we were still exclaiming over how great Loretta looked when we heard a car door slam and looked out the window to see . . . *Lester!*

"Lester!" I shrieked to the others.

"Tell him we're upstairs packing!" Dad said, racing for the stairs.

"Put the food away!" yelled Sylvia.

"Quick! What's the story line?" Loretta asked me.

"He's supposed to be driving Dad and Sylvia to

Dulles—they're on their way to London—and I'm supposed to be staying with Liz while they're gone," I said.

Gwen and Liz and I were already zapping the platters of sandwiches into the cold oven, the dishwasher, the cupboards. The macaroni salad went under the sink, the chocolate cakes in the fridge. . . .

We heard the screen door open, and then Loretta opened the front door before Lester could.

"Lester!" she cried.

He stared at her incredulously. "Loretta?"

"I just stopped by to see your dad and found that everybody's leaving!" she said. "They're going to London."

"Yeah, I'm driving them to the airport," said Les. "What about you? How *are* you?"

"Oh, Les, I could talk all night," Loretta said. "Do you really want to hear? I'm fine, and— Here! Sit down a minute. Your dad's still packing and I'm leaving soon, but, hey! You look great! What's with you? You don't live here anymore, do you?"

Lester looked around uncertainly as he sat down at one end of the couch.

"Liz and I are making dinner to take over to her house for our friends," I said, poking my head through the kitchen doorway. "I'd give you some,

Les, but we're sort of having a party over there."

"It's okay," he said. "I'll talk with Loretta."

I slipped back into the kitchen as Loretta chattered on.

"What are we going to *do*?" I whispered in a panic to Gwen, Liz, and Pamela. "Should I go outside and direct people around to the back before they can knock?"

"He'll hear car doors slamming and people talking. He'll know something's up," said Pamela.

Loretta must have been giving him an account of every day of her life since he saw her last. He was probably feeling trapped all over again.

Then the doorbell rang a second time. I answered to find Rosalind and her older brother Billy.

"Lester's here, but he doesn't suspect anything yet," I whispered as I motioned wildly toward the living room. Rosalind nodded.

"Oh, hi, Roz!" I said, louder. "We're about ready to go over to Elizabeth's. We're making dinner here to take over."

She didn't miss a beat. "Want me to carry something?"

And then Les saw her brother. "Bill!" he exclaimed, getting up.

"Heeeey! Drummer boy!" Bill said. "What are you doing here? I just dropped Roz off, but I didn't know you lived here too."

"I don't," said Les. "I've got an apartment in Takoma Park, but I'm driving my dad and step-mother to the airport." They shook hands. "Sit down. I've got some time yet," Lester said, and introduced Loretta to Bill.

More shaking of hands. But the doorbell rang again.

This time Lester's housemates—Paul and George—walked in, and they had old Mr. Watts with them.

"Where's the cake?" the old man asked loudly, and, seeing Lester, he joked, "Never mind the birth-day boy. Bring on the cake!" And then Les knew.

Dad and Sylvia came downstairs, laughing.

"You *guys*!" Lester said, slapping his forehead.

"The trip's off," Dad said, grinning. "We decided we'd rather stay here and help celebrate."

"I can't believe you pulled this off," Lester said.

"We can't either," I told him. "What do you mean, showing up almost an hour early?"

"I was hungry," Les confessed. "I figured what-ever you had in your fridge had to be more than I've got in mine."

And did we party! Lester's baseball buddies came next, and soon everyone was out in the backyard feasting on sandwiches and salads. I'd put on one of Lester's favorite CDs that was a favorite of mine, too.

It was fun having Lester's friends around. I hadn't met any of the people he hung out with at school and only a couple of the guys he played ball with. It's weird in a way. It's like seeing a whole other part of your brother—a different personality, even—and you have to remind yourself that he has a life completely separate from yours.

When guests found out that Lester and Bill used to play in a band together, they demanded a concert. Bill had a couple of acoustic guitars in the car, so he and Les performed right there in the backyard. It was only a couple of numbers, but I could tell that Les was enjoying himself.

A group of guys were gathered in one corner of the yard, beers in hand, laughing and telling stories about Lester. George Palamas had stayed about forty-five minutes and then taken Mr. Watts back home. But Paul Sorenson sat on a folding chair at the edge of the group, looking about as stiff and out of place as a paper clip in a bowl of rubber bands. He'd smile from time to time at something one of the guys said, but he didn't know any of them, and I could tell he wasn't really a part of the conversation. He glanced at his watch once, propped his left ankle over his right knee, coughed, and reversed it.

He was very tall, gangly, with blondish hair.

Decent-looking but too serious, I thought, for his own good. Maybe it was because I knew he was feeling out of place, or because he was shy, but before Pamela could notice and grab him, I went over. Someone had put on a polka.

"Come on," I said, reaching out my hand. "Let's dance."

Paul looked up. Looked startled. "No," he said, laughing a little. "I can't." He leaned back away from me slightly, a faint blush spreading on his face.

"Sure you can. I'll teach you," I said, tugging at his hand.

I really hadn't meant to embarrass him, but I realized then that I had. He had to choose between the awkwardness of refusing me or a possible humiliation out on the lawn. Liz and Gwen and Rosalind were already dancing, while Pamela tried to sneak a beer. I smiled at Paul encouragingly, and he gave in. Liz saw us and mouthed, *Go, Alice!*

I took Paul's hands, facing him, and waited for the beat. "AND one two three AND one two three . . ." I said as he watched my feet. "It's sort of like a gallop across the yard," I told him.

Gamely, he gave it a try. He tripped once or twice, but then he caught on, and we went hopping across the grass, first one foot, then the other.

I heard a little chuckle come from his throat as we almost collided with Dad and Sylvia, and I could feel him relax just by the way he held me.

"Isn't this great weather for a party?" I said.

"Wonderful," said Paul.

What would it be like, I wondered, to date "an older man"? Paul was probably older than Lester, even. What would we talk about if he took me out? If we were with another couple? I wondered if what Lester talked about at our dinner table was just watered-down ideas he thought I could understand, or if guys like Paul Sorenson liked some of the same things I did.

The polka was over, and we were both breathing hard. Paul's forehead glistened, and he grinned at me.

"Well, that was fun!" he said.

"We did all right!" I said, smiling back. For a second or two I didn't release his hands, even when I felt them relax. Was I *crushing* on him? I wondered. Lester's *roommate*? I'd been to his apartment! I'd seen him in his stocking feet! I'd seen a hole in his T-shirt!

"Enjoy the party," I said, reluctantly letting go of his hands and my daydream both.

Later, the way Les lit into that chocolate cake, it appeared to me that he still had a lot of reasons to live and wasn't going to stay depressed too much longer. Besides, Dad told me later, twenty-four is still too young for a guy to settle down. Especially Lester.

I wanted to connect with my relatives more—not just when I had a question or a favor to ask—so the next morning I called Uncle Milt and Aunt Sally, just to tell them about the party.

"What's the matter?" Aunt Sally asked as soon as she heard my voice. With my aunt, it's always an emergency if I call first.

"Nothing! I just called to say hello before I get too busy at school," I said. "And I wanted to tell you about the surprise party we gave for Lester."

"Oh, tell me about it!" she said, relieved. "What fun! My goodness, he's twenty-four years old! I *married* at twenty-four."

I was about to say that Lester would have married too if Tracy had said yes, but I stopped myself in time. I told her how he thought he was coming to drive Dad and Sylvia to the airport, but he had been the second person to arrive, and how we had to hide all the food.

It was wonderful to hear Aunt Sally laugh. I wished I could have been in Chicago in person, telling her all this, sitting there in their living room between her and Uncle Milt, laughing the way we used to when I was little.

"That reminds me of a party your mother and I gave when she was twelve and I was sixteen," Aunt Sally said. "We decided to give a come-as-you-are party for our friends. Everyone was supposed to show up wearing whatever they had on when they got our phone call. And of course we made our calls early in the morning or late in the evening, hoping to catch friends in their pajamas."

"And did you?" I asked.

"Worse than that," said Aunt Sally. "Oh my goodness, we opened the door to one guest, and all he had around him was a towel. He said he'd gotten out of the shower to answer the phone when we called, and that's all he was wearing."

I laughed.

"I tell you, we spent the whole evening trying to figure out if he had any shorts on under that towel, and it was a party to remember."

"Wow!" I said. "Aunt Sally, you were hot! It's nice that you and Mom did things together even though there was a four-year age difference between you."

"Oh, she was my precious baby sister," Aunt Sally said. "I was so protective of Marie. And . . . in the end . . . I couldn't protect her at all, could I?" I heard Aunt Sally sigh. "But you know, the more protective I was of her, the more . . .

adventurous she became. Mother always said that half the gray hair on her head came from old age and the other half came from raising Marie."

"Really?" This was news to me. "What did Mom do?"

"Oh, things like hitchhiking once with a girl-friend to the next town. Dad was really angry about that. And the time she rode a bike through downtown Chicago. And the time she spent the night on our roof. . . ."

It suddenly occurred to me that my mother had had a more exciting life than I had. It must have seemed that way to Aunt Sally, too, because she began to backpedal. "Listen, Alice, I only told you these things as a cautionary tale. Don't you go try-ing them yourself. Marie had more sense after she grew up. We just didn't know whether she'd *live* to grow up, that's all."

"Why didn't you tell me all this before?" I asked.

"For the very reason that we wanted *you* to live to grow up too," she said.

"I love everything you tell me," I said. "I never get tired of hearing about her."

"I know," said Aunt Sally. "And I never get tired of telling."

* * *

A few minutes after I hung up the phone, it rang again. Sylvia was raking leaves in the backyard, and I saw her look toward the house.

"I'll get it," I called out to her, and answered. It was Dad.

"Alice, I've been trying to get you for the last ten minutes," he said.

"I was on the phone with Aunt Sally," I explained.

"Well, I just got a call from Howard," he told me, meaning one of his twin brothers down in Tennessee. "Dad's very sick, and I think we should all fly down to Tennessee this afternoon."

We?

"Uh . . . how bad is it?" I asked in a small voice.

"It's congestive heart failure. The doctors don't expect him to live more than a few days, at the most." I heard a catch in my father's voice.

"Oh, Dad!" I cried.

"I've already called Lester, and we've got plane reservations for the four of us leaving National at two thirty. Paul Sorenson's going to drive us to the airport. Would you ask Sylvia to pack for me? I have to finish something up here, and then I'll be home."

"Y-Yes," I said. "Dad, I'm so sorry."

I went out on the back porch and told Sylvia. She left the rake where she'd dropped it and started for the house. At one that afternoon we were standing in line for our boarding passes at the airport.

18

And Life Goes On

I'd wanted a reunion. I'd wanted the whole family to gather, but not like this. I'd imagined Uncle Howard and Uncle Harold, Aunt Vivian, Aunt Linda, and Aunt Marge all coming to Maryland for Lester and Tracy's wedding, bringing Gramps with them in his wheelchair.

Instead, we sat on vinyl seats in the airport, watching planes come in and take off. I wished Dad would talk to me, but he seemed locked inside himself, not saying much to anyone. Sylvia didn't talk much either. She held Dad's hand, and now and then she patted his arm. I was stuck with Lester, who had brought one of his philosophy textbooks with him and was writing notes in the margins.

I wished we were driving to Tennessee in our car, me curled up in the backseat with my CD player. On the train. A bus, even. I felt like my life was shaky right now, like I needed something solid beneath me. My thoughts traveled back and forth from Grandpa McKinley dying down in Tennessee to the lines of people moving through the doors and down the ramps to their planes. How did those huge planes, weighing tons, make it up in the air, anyway? I never did understand it exactly.

An attendant was moving toward the door now and took the rope away from the entrance to the ramp. "Flight 3651 to Nashville," she said to one section of the waiting area.

People began gathering up their things. Lester closed his book and stood up. Dad and Sylvia stood up too and reached for their bags.

It felt as though there were a balloon in my chest growing larger and larger. I couldn't understand it. It was a strange, hollow feeling I'd never had before, though it was something like the dread I used to experience when facing the deep end of the swimming pool. *Thumpa . . . thumpa . . . thumpa* went my heart as I followed them to the doorway and showed my boarding pass.

I felt weak, and my hands were cold. I'd never been on a plane before that I could remember. The only movies I'd seen about planes were disaster movies. Dad and Sylvia had gone on ahead, and I was tagging along behind Lester.

"Les," I said in a quavery voice, "do pilots ever

drink and fly?" He turned and raised one eyebrow at me, but I scurried up alongside him. "*Do* they?" I insisted.

"They're not supposed to have a drink within eight hours of a flight," he said.

"'Not supposed to' isn't the same as 'don't,'" I said.

"Well, if they do, they can lose their jobs," said Lester.

Why would that matter if the plane went down? I thought. They'd certainly lose their jobs *then*. We followed the ramp to the door of the plane. Two flight attendants stood just inside and smiled at us. Never mind the attendants, I decided. The door to the cockpit was open a few inches, and I inhaled as we passed. No booze that I could detect.

Les and I had seats by the emergency door a few rows behind Dad and Sylvia. A businessman in a pin-striped suit sat in the window seat reading a newspaper. I slid in next to him, and Lester took the aisle seat.

Passengers were putting their carry-on bags in the overhead compartments, and attendants moved up and down the aisles to help out. The FASTEN SEAT BELTS sign was on, and I buckled up, the dread in my chest growing stronger and stronger. There was still time to get off if I wanted.

Should I? Life or death. Which should I choose? My breathing came fast.

Lester glanced over at me. "You okay?" he asked.

I couldn't answer.

"You've been on a plane before, haven't you, Al?" he asked.

"When would I have been on a plane?" I squeaked. "You've lived with me practically my whole life. Did you ever see me get on a plane?"

"Guess not," said Lester. He fastened his seat belt and opened his philosophy book again.

The attendants came down the aisle closing the doors to the overhead bins and checking seat belts. Then they took seats themselves up front. That meant the plane doors were closed and locked. It was too late to get off. Now I *wanted* the doors to be locked. Double locked! Had anyone checked the emergency door? I wondered. The plane started to move. It was backing away from the terminal and slowly turning itself around, like some huge prehistoric beast. Then it moved onto the runway.

I reached over and grabbed Lester's hand. Surprisingly, he didn't shake me off. It helped to connect with someone, but I felt my body shake.

"Lester," I mewed pitifully, "if we crash and you live and I don't, I want you to forgive every awful thing I ever said to you."

"We're not going to crash, Al."

The pilot began to rev the engines. The sound grew louder and louder. The plane began to move, faster and faster. I pushed back stiffly against the seat and glanced sideways at the man by the window. He was still reading his newspaper. How could you read a newspaper when your body was hurtling down a runway at 150 miles an hour?

I felt the plane lifting off. What if we were too heavy? What if something fell off? What if we couldn't get up enough speed and—?

Thunk.

"Lester!" I yelped. "What was that?"

"The landing gear retracting, Al. Calm down, will you?" he whispered.

"What about birds?"

"What *about* them?"

"Fall's coming, Lester! They're migrating! What if a goose flies in our engine and—?"

"Al . . ."

"What if the emergency door flies open and I get sucked out of the plane and—?"

The man next to me couldn't hold back any longer: "Then we will have a much more pleasant flight," he said, and returned to his paper.

That shut me up. My fingernails were digging into Lester's arm so hard that they were leaving marks. When I could see that the trees and houses were far below us, I released my grip and closed my eyes. Whatever was going to happen would happen. I couldn't get up, couldn't get off, and I resigned myself to my fate.

And strangely enough, I began to relax. I guess it was the choice that had bothered me—whether I should go or not. Now that it was out of my hands, I could feel my breathing slow.

I waited until the sound of the plane's engines dropped to a constant hum, and after five minutes or so, the FASTEN SEAT BELTS light went off. I looked around. People were reading or sleeping or talking with each other. Nobody was panicky and plastered against his seat back. No one had his head buried in his lap. The attendants were smiling. The pilot was saying, "Good afternoon" and telling us what the weather was like in Nashville.

Les was reading his philosophy book again.

"Les," I said, "what do you think is the matter with me?"

"Emotionally, mentally, or physically?" he asked.

"Any or all," I said.

"I think you are emotionally overwrought, mentally challenged, and physically . . . uh . . ."

"Never mind," I said, and jabbed him in the side.

"I think that you were having a mini panic attack about a new experience and that when the flight's over, you'll add it to your list of fun things to do."

"Panic attacks?"

"No. Flying."

"Were you ever afraid of something?" I asked him. "Really afraid?"

"Yeah, public speaking. When I had to give a report in class, I just about lost it. I'd be sick to my stomach a day or two before the big event. Wouldn't sleep at all the night before."

"What were you afraid would happen?"

"Oh . . . that I'd lose my voice or sweat a river or forget something."

"Did it happen?"

"I mispronounced a word or two. Lost my place a couple of times. But after a while I noticed that almost *every*body mispronounced something or got mixed up at some point, and it was no big deal."

I finally took my history book out of my bag and read a chapter, or tried to. My mind kept drifting to Patrick, the way he and his parents had flown all over the whole world, practically. I wondered if he was maybe reading this same chapter at this exact moment. I was thinking about the way we usually sat together in class now. Wondering, I guess, if it meant anything.

"Les," I said, "seeing as how Patrick and I met for the first time in sixth grade and then went out for more than two years, do you think it means anything that we're sitting beside each other now in World History?"

"Yeah," said Lester. "It means that all of the other seats were taken."

I felt easier when the plane began to descend into the Nashville airport. It just seemed more natural for a plane to be coming down and landing than for it to be rising up in the air and trying to fly. But soon we were on the ground, and people were unfastening their seat belts and opening the overhead compartments.

"Welcome to Nashville," the flight attendant said as we moved toward the door with our bags.

The cockpit door was open, and a pilot was standing there.

"Thank you for a great trip," I gushed. "You got us up so smoothly, and we hardly had any turbulence! It was a very safe landing, and I—"

"Stifle it, Al," Lester whispered behind me.

"Thank you, thank you," the pilot said, smiling. "You're welcome to ride with us anytime."

Uncle Howard was waiting for us at the baggage claim. He and Dad embraced and held it for ten seconds or so without a word. Finally Dad asked, "How is he?"

"Still holding on," Uncle Howard said.

"Is everyone there?"

"Yes."

Uncle Howard looked a lot like Dad, an older version, of course. His hair was mostly gray, and the skin sagged a little on the cheeks and under the eyes, but he had the same smile. He turned toward me then and hugged me, and I thought what a fraud I was. I didn't want to be there at all.

I hate sickness and pain and throwing up and getting dizzy. I'd been working in a hospital as a candy striper when my favorite teacher, Mrs. Plotkin, died. I've hated hospitals ever since, with their sounds and smells and stretchers and tubes and people running around in white coats and green scrubs with little flecks of blood on their running shoes. I hate seeing patients standing in hallways wearing cotton gowns that are supposed to be fastened in the back but aren't. I hate seeing people cry. I hate hearing doctors' names announced again and again over the speaker system, and you wonder if there's a patient dying somewhere and his doctor's down having coffee.

Most of all, I hate death, and don't even want to think about it. I've always felt as though Grandpa McKinley was sort of the wall between my own dad and death. That I didn't have to worry about Dad dying until *his* dad died. And now it was like

Dad was next in line. Except maybe Uncle Harold and Uncle Howard, being older, would go first.

"It was nice of you to come," Uncle Howard said, hugging Sylvia and shaking Lester's hand. "I wish it were a different occasion."

"We all do," said Sylvia.

How can everything look gloomy even when the sun is shining? How can even smiling people look sad? I didn't want to be in Nashville any more than I'd wanted to be on that plane, and yet . . . I looked at my dad sitting up there in the front seat beside Uncle Howard. How was it for *him*?

I was in the back between Les and Sylvia, and we didn't say a word all the way back to the house. We listened to the quiet conversation between Dad and his brother—when Grandpa had stopped eating, when he'd last had water, what the doctor had said. . . . "Resting comfortably" kept coming into the conversation.

We got out at Uncle Harold and Aunt Vivian's yellow frame house and went inside. Uncle Harold looks a lot like his twin, of course, only thinner. He smiled and said each of our names as he gave us a hug: "Alice . . . Ben . . . Sylvia . . . Lester." And finally, "Come on in."

My three aunts hovered there in the living

room, waiting their turn to hug us—Aunt Vivian, Aunt Linda, Howard's wife, and Aunt Marge, who had been married to my uncle Charlie for only two days before he died. In the background a comedy show was playing on the TV, and I wondered how anyone could be laughing in a house where someone was dying. It seemed surreal. Finally somebody turned it off.

"So good to *see* you!" said Aunt Linda, hugging me hard in her big arms.

"We're so glad you're here," said Aunt Vivian.

"So am I," said Dad.

"Dad wakes up for a few minutes at a time, then slips off again," Uncle Harold said. "Right now he's napping, but you can go up if you like."

"Yes, I'd like to see him," said Dad.

So did I. To tell the truth, I wanted it over with.

When you're somewhere you don't want to be, I discovered, it's like things are moving in slow motion. I found myself counting the number of steps upstairs, studying the grapevine pattern on the wallpaper, listening for sounds from the sickroom. . . .

Everything was quiet except for the raggedy sounds of Gramps's breathing. There he was in bed, looking so much smaller than I had remembered him, like a twelve-year-old boy. His left hand, lying on top of the light blanket, looked so thin and withered, like a claw almost, and I heard Dad suck in his breath when he saw him.

We went to the bed. Dad leaned over and touched the side of Gramps's face, smoothed the wisps of white hair on his forehead. I tried not to look at my dad's face, but I couldn't help myself. There were tears in his eyes, and then there were tears in mine.

Uncle Harold and Aunt Vivian had come upstairs with us. Lester and Sylvia, too.

"The doctor was by around one and said it's probably a matter of hours—a day or two at most," Uncle Harold whispered.

"I'll stay as long as necessary," said Dad. "Let me sit with him awhile—give you a break. I'll come down and get you if he wakes up."

"I'll stay," said Aunt Vivian. "Why don't you men go talk?"

"No," said Dad. "Let me."

I figured Dad wanted time alone with his father, so I followed the others downstairs. I felt like a spectator, sitting in the living room while my uncles and aunts made small talk with Les and Sylvia.

"Probably hard for Ben to leave the store on short notice," Uncle Howard said.

"Oh, he has capable help," Sylvia told him. "It's good for him to know he's not indispensable. And

I'm glad he got the chance to be here with his father."

"A hundred and one years old!" said Aunt Marge. "Think of that! We should all be so lucky."

"How's the thesis coming, Lester?" Uncle Harold asked. "You'll feel like a ten-ton weight is off your shoulders when it's finished, I'll bet."

"I'll feel like a weight's off my shoulders after I get a job," said Les. "You don't see many want ads in the newspaper for a philosopher."

We ate pound cake and drank cold sweetened tea.

"Could I take some up to Dad?" I asked.

"Of course," said Aunt Marge, and fixed up a little tray.

Upstairs Dad was still sitting by Gramps's bed, just watching.

"Dad," I said softly. "This is for you."

He turned. "Thanks," he said. "Just put it there on the nightstand."

I set the tray down. I wanted so much to say something comforting, but I didn't know what. "This is awfully sad," I said at last.

"Yes," he said. "It is."

"Do you suppose he's in pain?"

"No. The doctor doesn't think so."

"Do you want me to stay here with you?"

"I think it would be better if you go downstairs

and chat with the others. We may give you a turn later, sitting up here."

"Sure," I said, but the thought of sitting alone with Gramps was even more unsettling than being on the plane.

Aunt Vivian let me help with dinner. There was a pot roast simmering on the stove, the aroma of potatoes and onions, and I set to work making the salad. It was good to have something to do, to feel useful.

"Go get your dad, Lester," Aunt Linda said. "I'll go up in a minute and sit with Gramps."

Dad came down then, and we sat around the oval table in the big old-fashioned dining room with the dark woodwork and family pictures on the walls.

"It's not often we get the chance to have dinner with you," said Uncle Howard, beaming at me. "Alice, you've got your mother's coloring, all right. Your hair and your eyes look just like Marie's. What a fine young lady you're getting to be, growing up there in Silver Sprangs." It always comes out "Sprangs" when he says it. I smiled back.

They talked then about the kind of memorial service they had planned for Gramps.

"There are no friends of his left," said Uncle Harold. "He's outlived them all. So we thought we'd keep it simple—his favorite hymn, favorite scripture. . . ."

"What's his favorite scripture?" asked Sylvia.

"First Corinthians, thirteen," said Uncle Howard.

"That's my favorite too," Dad said.

The grown-ups sat at the table a long time talking then, so I got up and walked slowly around the dining room, studying each picture on the walls.

There was Grandma, who I'd never met, and Grandpa, standing stiffly out in the yard of a tall, narrow house, perhaps the first house they lived in after they were married. I knew it was Gramps because someone had written his name and his bride's in ink in one corner.

Another photo of Howard and Harold posing for their high school graduation pictures. Of Howard in his barbershop with a son I don't remember. Here was Dad playing the violin with Aunt Vivian at the piano. Dad and Mom's wedding picture, just like the one at home—Mom in a simple ivory dress with a spray of baby's breath in her hair.

I moved to the other side of the china cabinet to see the photos over there, many of cousins I'd never met. I smiled at a picture of Lester and me at some kind of fair. I couldn't have been more than two years old, sitting on a pony, and Les, at ten, leading it around a pony ring, looking bored. I turned and looked at him, watching me from across the table. I pointed to the picture, and he rolled his eyes. I grinned.

There were photos of people I didn't know, and one of Uncle Charlie and Aunt Marge leaving for their honeymoon. A picture of Dad and Sylvia dancing at their wedding reception. Gramps celebrating his ninetieth birthday—who would have thought he'd live another eleven years?

There was history here all over the walls. There were memories connecting us to these warm, loving people down in Tennessee, whether we saw them very often or not.

I went into the living room to check out the family Bible I'd seen on an end table. I looked in the front to find First Corinthians and turned to the passage that was Dad's favorite:

> Though I speak with the tongues of men and of angels, and have not charity, I am become as sounding brass, or a tinkling cymbal. And though I have the gift of prophecy, and understand all mysteries, and all knowledge; and though I have all faith, so that I could remove mountains, and have not charity, I am nothing. . . .

Aunt Marge came in after a while and sat down beside me on the couch.

"Charity?" I asked.

"Love," said Aunt Marge. She put one arm around me and squeezed my shoulder. After I had read the whole of the chapter and closed the Bible, Aunt Marge got out some scrapbooks and showed me more pictures of the family, including snapshots of her and my uncle Charlie.

"How long were you sad after he died?" I asked. "Does it last forever?"

She thought about that a moment. "I'm sad whenever I think about his dying and all that we missed, but I don't think about it all the time," she answered. "Mostly I remember the good times we had before we married and how much I like being part of this family now. They just took me right in."

I looked over at my relatives there at the big table in the dining room. I felt a lump growing larger in my throat. "My problem is that I don't remember many happy days with my mother because I don't remember her that well at all," I said.

"I didn't know you then, so I can't help," she said. "But this is what family is for. Lots of memories are stored in your other aunts and uncles, and you just ask them to tell you every single thing they remember about Marie. They'll help you fill up those empty spaces in your head."

I thought about my extended family, strung out

all across the country—my familiar relatives in Tennessee and Chicago. My new not-so-familiar relatives in Albuquerque and Seattle. I liked that we could smile and laugh together, even with Gramps dying upstairs. That it didn't mean the end of being happy.

Aunt Linda called down that Gramps was waking up—did we want to come and see him?

This time we all went up, and Dad sat down again in the chair beside the bed.

"Dad?" he said, leaning forward. "Do you know who I am?"

For fifteen seconds or so, Gramps stared at Dad and his lips moved a little. His fingers fluttered on his chest. Then he smiled just a little and looked excited. "B-B-Ben!" he said, his breath raggedy.

Dad put one hand over his father's. "I came to see you, Dad. I just got here a little while ago."

Gramps's eyes grew wider. "Ben . . . Ben . . . ," he said again, and smiled. Saliva gathered in the corners of his mouth. "How . . . how are . . . things?"

"Things are fine with me, Dad. Work is going well, and I've brought Sylvia and Lester and Alice with me."

"Lester?" said Gramps, and moved his head slightly.

Lester stepped up to the bedside where Gramps

could see him. He bent down and touched him on the shoulder. "Hi, Gramps," he said.

Gramps smiled even more broadly. "How . . . is . . . high school?" he asked, and the little gasps between each breath frightened me.

"I've graduated from high school," Lester said. "I'm in college now."

"College?"

"Yes. Graduate school. I'll be getting my master's next May, I hope."

"Gradu . . . ate school," said Gramps. He closed his eyes as though the effort of saying it had worn him out. Then he opened them again.

Dad motioned for me to come around the bed so Gramps could see me, too.

"Hello, Gramps," I said. I bent down and kissed his forehead. It felt as cold and dry as an old book cover.

When I straightened up, though, his eyes looked at me in surprise. I wondered if I had really grown that much since he'd seen me at Dad's wedding. "Well!" he said. "Look . . . who's . . . here."

"Yes, I came too," I told him.

"Marie!" said Gramps. "Marie!"

Everyone was startled, and then . . . everyone began to smile. Sylvia too.

I decided that what I could do most for my

grandfather was to be whomever he wanted. I could tell from his voice, his smile, that my mother had been very dear to him, and I was glad that for now, I was her.

Dad gave up his chair by the bed temporarily and motioned me to sit down. I took his place, holding Gramps's bony hand in mine. I knew I'd cry later, but for now, I did my best to smile.

"You came!" said Gramps, giving my hand a tiny squeeze.

"Yes," I said. "And I'll stay as long as you want me to."

❀